Life After Death

by

Sharon Saracino

Max Logan Series, Book 2

Life After Death

Cover Art by *Debbie Taylor*

The Wild Rose Press, Inc.
PO Box 708
Adams Basin, NY 14410-0708
Visit us at www.thewildrosepress.com

Publishing History
First Fantasy Rose Edition, 2017
Previously published by Whiskey Creek Press, 2014
Print ISBN 978-1-5092-1543-0
Digital ISBN 978-1-5092-1544-7

Max Logan Series, Book 2
Published in the United States of America

My aching spine seemed to straighten

of its own accord as I recognized the calculated, feral gaze. My black wolf! I guess most people would find this discovery shocking and completely unbelievable but given recent events I'd been sucker punched into suspending disbelief. It was cool. I was down with it. No problem-o.

"Oh my God, you're a freaking werewolf?" I screeched, bounding from my chair and hobbling several long steps away from him.

I freely admit I'd spent a good deal of time feeling sorry for myself over the last few years. Following my death and victorious return to the land of the living, I'd worked really hard at pulling myself away from the precipice of the bottomless pit of self-pity. All things considered, I actually had a pretty good life. But honestly, trapped with a bum ankle in an isolated cabin in the middle of a freak blizzard with a Grim Reaper who was also a werewolf, while planning to cross the veil to the other side to rescue my ex-husband from a D.I.E.? Seriously, why me?

"Hellhound, actually," he growled, rising to his feet. My back was against a wall, literally. I had nowhere to go. Then again, at least I had a stable surface against which to support my knocking knees. Glass half full, Max.

Praise for Sharon Saracino

Ms. Saracino's Max Logan Series was a 2015 Paranormal Romance Guild Reviewers Choice Paranormal Series Nominee.

~*~

Her book, *LIFE AFTER DEATH*, was a 2015 RONE Award Paranormal Nominee and 2015 EPIC Award Finalist.

~*~

"Good and evil battle, with good winning, but not without a cost and a wicked twist that will have the reader hungry for the previous book as well as additional imaginings Ms. Saracino chooses to serve up."

~InD'Tale Magazine

~*~

SMITTEN WITH DEATH was a 2016 RONE Award Paranormal nominee, a 2015 PRG Reviewer's Choice Winner for Best Paranormal Romance Novel, and the 2016 Maple Leaf Award Winner for Best Novel.

~*~

"…a fabulously entertaining read that has this reviewer wanting to read the entire series and searching for chocolate-covered Arabica beans!"

~InD'Tale Magazine

Dedication

Dedicated to everyone who has ever had to bend,
but not break.

Chapter One

"Good morning, Maxine."

The overwhelming lethargy in my limbs told me it was too early for consciousness let alone conversation. The bright radiance I discerned through my closed eyelids argued it might be well after noon. Anyone who knows me is aware that waking me from a peaceful slumber is akin to signing their own death warrant. Therefore, I assumed the cheery voice must be talking to some other girl named Maxine. I snuggled farther down into my cocoon of fifteen-hundred count Egyptian cotton bed linens and tried to fall back to sleep.

"Rise and shine, Cupcake. We need to talk."

Oddly, the voice sounded familiar. Since I live alone and my grossly overweight feline, Sir Chicken Caesar, has never acquired the gift of gab, I deduced I must be dreaming. The sharp prodding in my ribs felt real enough however, and the voice came from somewhere to my right as opposed to somewhere in my head. I reluctantly cracked one eyelid open and squinted against the blinding glare.

"*Alicia?*" The official Superintendent of Spiritual Impediment, aka SSI, lay stretched out comfortably on the side of the bed occasionally occupied by my ex-husband and current boyfriend, Roger-the-Proctologist. Roger was presently in Colorado for a two week medical seminar related to diseases and bodily functions I had no desire to examine too closely.

Have I mentioned his specialty is Proctology?

I squinted in displeasure at the garishly green numbers on my alarm clock. It read two-oh-five a.m. If there's one thing I really hate, it's waking up at stupid o'clock. The annoying luminosity I mistook for the early afternoon sunlight came, in fact, from Alicia who, when the mood struck her, could glow like a radioactive Christmas tree—on steroids. I hadn't seen or heard from her since that happy day months ago when I'd been relieved of my duties as SSI. I'd been temporarily obligated to assume the position to regain my status among the living after my untimely Death in Error (D.I.E.) caused by an overeager Grim Reaper in Training (G.R.I.T). Turns out the bureaucrats in the afterlife are quite enamored with acronyms. Who knew?

Anyway, I'm not complaining. Not that I have anything against Alicia personally, but I prefer to relegate that period of my life—or death, depending on how I choose to look at it on any given day—to the been-there-done-that file. I mean, c'mon, wouldn't you? I've never shared my life after death after life experience with anyone. Not even Roger. After the fact, even *I* wasn't completely convinced the entire episode was real. In the first place, my black Italian marble shower and I came together quite dramatically in a completely involuntary manner that cracked my skull hard enough to scramble my brain into a convincing three dimensional hallucination easily misinterpreted as a near death experience. Secondly, who in their right mind would believe me? Sure, I'd emerged from the experience a kinder and gentler Max Logan, filled with insight and forgiveness, ready to own up to my own part in the misery that had become my everyday existence. However, those who knew me best were far more likely to attribute it to a temporary psychotic break than any supernatural intervention.

"Alicia, I'm going back to sleep for at least the next five hours. I am returning to the place where I'm always thin, never run out of money, and I'm sitting on a private beach with hot cabana boys who bring me exotic cocktails with little paper umbrellas. Do not attempt to wake me again or my stuffed bear will attack," I threatened in a sleep thickened voice.

"You don't have a stuffed bear," my uninvited visitor pointed out.

"Totally irrelevant, Glow Girl. Come back later," I grumbled, burrowing even deeper into my luxury bed linens. The sheets had been a gift from my slightly extravagant younger half-sister, Denise. I didn't share my sister's purchasing compulsion, but I've come to understand it is one of the ways in which Denise shows affection. Since I seem to be the recipient of nearly as much of her profligate spending as her twin bundles of joy, Mick and Vick, I've come to the conclusion she must really love me. "And turn the lights off, while you're at it."

Alicia's annoying brilliance immediately dimmed a few thousand kilowatts. "Sorry, apparently you aren't a morning person," she laughed, sounding not the least bit offended. Could I possibly be losing my touch? I offend people all the time. I've actually been known to offend more people before breakfast than some people manage to do all day.

"But I really do need to talk to you." She nudged my backside with a pointy-toe. "Really, Max. It's important. C'mon, girlie, get the lead out. I even made coffee," she continued in a cajoling sing-song voice that crawled right under my skin and made the hair on the back of my neck stand at attention.

"Roses are red, violets are blue, I've got five fingers on each hand, Alicia, and the middle ones are for you," I groused. Whatever her other talents, the woman apparently could not take a hint. To say I wasn't a morning person might be something of a gross understatement. I'm pretty sure you can find it carved in stone somewhere. Truthfully, in my opinion the moron who first assumed the words *good* and *morning* belonged in the same sentence deserved to be slapped in the face. Hard.

On the other hand, the persistent sparkler *had* mentioned the magic word—coffee. I would like to pause and take a moment here to offer my deepest thanks to whoever saw the coffee bean growing wild on a bush somewhere and thought *Hey, if we crush that puppy and boil it with water it will be AWESOME! That* guy was a freakin' genius. Just saying.

"Still have the charming little habit of speaking your mind, I see," Alicia laughed again.

Okay, so maybe death had taught me a lot of things, but I still found speaking my mind hurt a lot less than biting my tongue. Most of the time, anyway. Hey, I'm working on it, okay? I inched the top sheet down the bridge of my nose just far enough to take a peek.

Alicia lounged on her back, her arms folded behind her head on Roger-the-Proctologist's sometimes pillow, staring happily at the ceiling. Her legs were bent at the knees, one denim clad limb slung over the other. She looked altogether too comfortable, bright-eyed, and beautiful for this un-holy hour of the morning. Note to self: the law frowns upon placing a pillow over someone's face and holding it there until they stop struggling.

May I reiterate I am not a morning person?

With a deep sigh expelled deliberately loud enough to communicate my irritation, I threw back the sheet and slid gracefully from the bed. Fine, maybe my oversized T-shirt rode up in the back exposing my somewhat chunky butt, and one ankle turned when my feet hit the floor causing me to wave my arms in a wild propeller-like motion in an attempt to maintain my balance. You have your definition of graceful, and I have mine. Coordination and I have never been friends.

Alicia bounced from Roger's side of the bed, and landed on her dainty kitten heels with nary a wobble. I bet the bitch could walk in stilettos without breaking an ankle, too. She offered me a satisfied smirk. "See, that wasn't so bad. Now go and freshen up. I'll pour you a nice cup of coffee."

I hobbled toward my decadently luxurious bathroom, glaring at her from the crusty slits that passed for my eyes at two in the morning, while firmly reminding myself prison orange is not my color. I reached around the corner to flick on the bathroom light. I squinted into the mirror, ignoring the fine network of wrinkles that had begun to attach themselves to the corners of my eyes and lips. Not to mention the fifteen or so extra pounds I carried around on my thirty-six year old body. Everyone knows as we get older we acquire more and more information in our head. At my age my head just couldn't hold any more and it started to spread out and fill up the rest of me. Therefore, I've concluded I'm not overweight, I'm simply incredibly intelligent. Rationalization is a lifestyle.

No matter how important Alicia's reason for dropping by, she would have to wait a few minutes. The only thing that had an ice cube's chance in hell of waking me up at this hour, aside from a naked George Clooney with a bottle of tequila in his hand and a rose between his teeth, was a shower. I reached into the glass enclosed Italian marble cubicle and activated my absolute favorite thing in the entire apartment, my Chastings Corque Corian Square Ceiling Mount Showerhead. Of course, the biggest drawback to the shameless luxury of Italian marble is the fact that when combined with soap, shampoo, and water, it has a tendency to become the slick equivalent of an Olympic ice skating rink. I know this because I am a reasonably intelligent woman. I also know because several months ago, my ungainly attempt to retrieve my cotton crocheted bath puff totally soaked with water and oozing with soap by grasping it between my toes, led to my untimely and temporary demise.

Long story short? Fell in the shower, fatally cracked my skull, woke up dead, used my mad skills and superior knowledge of the Kubler-Ross stages of grief, found a loop hole, blackmailed the Director of the Office of Central Processing, and bargained my way back into the land of the living.

I stepped into the stall and pointedly refrained from looking down at the tacky little vinyl skid-proof fishies stuck to the floor of my lovely shower. Following my death by soap, I'd reluctantly applied the vinyl monstrosities, in direct opposition to my aesthetic sensibilities.

What? I do so have aesthetic sensibilities!

I capitulated in the matter of the sticky fish because I fervently wanted to avoid a repeat visit to the afterlife. In addition, I just as fervently needed to put an end to the incessant nagging of Stepmother Gail. She still hasn't quite recovered from the sight of my marble split scalp and the gallons of blood gushing forth. Turns out she likes me, she really likes me. Who knew? Her heart's in the right place, and I appreciate the concern, but vinyl sticky fish? Seriously? So not me. Though my bright idea to conceal their little white fishy tails with black nail polish did render them slightly less noticeable against the marble.

Sometimes my own brilliance simply astounds me.

The shower didn't wake me up half as much as I'd hoped, but at least I now had the ability to walk a straight line. I performed a half-hearted swipe and sop with one of my thick, and thankfully absorbent, Carrere Luxor Bath Towels, another Denise gift. Despite my best efforts, enough dampness persisted that my jeans and sweatshirt vehemently protested being donned at this early and unfamiliar hour by sticking and rolling stubbornly as I tried to force them over my moist skin.

Need I elaborate on how irritating that is?

It did not improve my mood in the least to hear the irksomely cheerful humming emanating from my open plan living room-kitchen-office-fine dining area. I'd heard whispered tales of the elusive Morning People. I'd relegated such nonsense to the realm of urban legend. Of course, considering the particulars of my temporary death and subsequent return to the land of the living, I guess I shouldn't be surprised to find the mythical creatures really do exist. I simply didn't understand why I should be the unfortunate schmuck forced to have one visited upon me.

I schlepped out of the bathroom and found Alicia had slipped off her shoes and made herself comfortable on my sofa. She sipped coffee from my favorite mug. I had the uncharitable thought I could truly learn to hate someone so perky and unintentionally pretty in the middle of the night. But, she *had* made coffee, so what the hell, more power to her.

Finally semi-lucid and awake, I gathered enough of my wits to wonder at the reason for Alicia's unexpected nocturnal visit. Unease swirled in my gut. As the SSI, Alicia is a go-between kind of supernatural social worker whose job is to rectify the unfinished business that might hinder recently departed spirits from advancing to the next phase of existence. Once her work is completed, the Grim Reaper severs the soul from its earthly tethers, and the spirit is able to move on. I had briefly filled in for Alicia while she took her maternity leave last year—following my untimely demise and as a condition of my return to the land of the living. Luckily for me, I knew how to recognize a weakness in the system and exploit the hell out of it. As I may have mentioned earlier, I'd consigned the entire experience to the been-there-done-that file and couldn't imagine why she suddenly turned up in my apartment out of the blue. Disquiet, something that should have shown up earlier if I'd had any sense, churned into true nausea as I realized whatever the reason, it probably couldn't be anything good.

I snagged my steaming mug from the counter where Alicia had left it, and eased down into the arm chair across from her. They couldn't revoke my return from the dead, could they? I'd lived up to my end of the bargain, such as it was. Of course I wouldn't put anything past that little weasel, Marvin Jenks, the Director of the Office of Central Processing.

"How's the baby?" I asked conversationally, selecting the least threatening topic I could think of.

"Oh." Alicia started as though she'd been somewhere else entirely. Given she possessed some funky supernatural superpowers, maybe she had been. "She's great, thanks. Growing like a weed."

"Uh, huh."

"So, I guess you're probably wondering why I'm here?"

"Uh, huh."

"Well, you remember when you died?" Alicia drawled. A thousand and one sarcastic comebacks sprang to mind and wrestled amongst themselves to hurry over my tongue and force themselves between my lips, but I judiciously remained silent. I'm told I have an attitude. I prefer to think I simply have a personality some people can't handle. I figured I could probably defend almost any smartass response that managed to escape my tightly compressed lips by prefacing it with *'ask a stupid question'. I mean, c'mon! I DIED! That wasn't likely to slip my mind anytime soon.*

"Uh, huh."

See how well I'm doing with that whole attitude thing?

"Well you might not realize this, but that whole episode was rather unusual." Alicia halted, seemingly reluctant to continue. Tough! I wasn't the one who woke *her* up in the middle of the night and wanted to bond. I sure as hell wasn't about to let her off the hook now that I was showered, shined, and shivering.

"Uh, huh."

Sparkling repartee, that's my specialty.

"First of all, you shouldn't have ended up in the Office of Central Processing." Alicia sat up straighter, and took a big sip of coffee.

"First of all, I shouldn't have ended up dead," I retorted sharply. "Your guy screwed up...big time."

"Point taken. However, the fact remains when all is said and done, you were able to come back and fill in for me. That should simply not have been possible."

"Just lucky I guess. Not everyone is as well versed in Kubler-Ross as I am." I smirked. None of Buddy-the-Inept's other accidental victims had been sent back. They'd all stayed on as permanent guests of the sweet hereafter. Thanks to my high school term paper, I knew Elizabeth Kubler-Ross documented five stages of grieving. When I found myself dead? I stubbornly kept my freshly showered and naked butt firmly planted in stage one: Denial with a capital D. I'll admit, I did let Anger with a capital A rear its ugly head occasionally. Can you blame me?

Fortuitously, I'd also easily recognized the growing anxiety of Marvin Jenks, thanks to my sister's obsession with amateur psychology. I also know everybody has an angle. I just had to figure out Marvin's and how I could work it to my advantage. And then my ship came steaming into port in the person of Buddy, the Grim-Reaper-In-Training who'd erroneously severed my soul.

Coincidentally, Buddy also turned out to be Marvin's nephew and it soon became apparent this wasn't Buddy's first royal screw up. Poor Buddy, attempting to appear so humble and apologetic. Yeah, I didn't buy it. Clearly, Marvin feared his unwise foray into nepotism might put his ass in a sling. Did my heart bleed for poor, perspiring Marvin and his family troubles? Hardly. Never one to waste an opportunity, I moved right on to the next step in the Kulber-Ross pecking order. Bargaining with a capital B. Hey, I'm not proud of it. Well, maybe I'm a *little* proud of it, but I wanted my life back, and so I made old Marv an OHCR—Offer He Couldn't Refuse.

Have I mentioned they're very big on acronyms in the afterlife? Marvin claims it saves time. Apparently there is a good deal of paperwork involved. But, I digress.

Alicia was out on maternity leave. Marvin desperately needed a temporary SSI. I desperately needed to resume my life. I scratched his back, and he scratched mine. Metaphorically speaking. Realistically, I wouldn't touch Marvin's back, or any other part of him, with a ten foot pole.

"No, you don't get it, Max. Regardless of your impressive mastery of Kubler-Ross, no average *human* should have been able to replace me. The corporeally challenged should not have been able to find *you*, and *you* should not have been able to accommodate *them*." Alicia sounded a little agitated. Maybe she should consider switching to decaf?

"Alicia, I'm not a moron. In fact, if you'll take note of the size of my hips, you'll realize I'm actually quite bright. I get it. But I haven't been cadaver catnip since you took over. All of that was only due to the temporary SSI superpowers Marvin gave me as part of our bargain. Once you took over...poof! No more transparent visitors with unresolved business. So what's your point?"

"The point is." Alicia drew a deep breath and paused. A pause so thick and portentous it almost became visible in the air. She remained silent for so long, I regretted asking that oh so itch-able question. Because when you have an itch, you scratch it. When you scratch an itch? You draw blood. And in this case, that blood would be mine. I just knew it.

"The point is," Alicia continued at last, "Marvin didn't give you any supernatural superpowers you didn't already possess. He doesn't have the authority. He made that bargain with you fully expecting you would fail."

"Why, that two faced rumple-suited rat boy!" I shouted hotly. "Wait a minute! What do you mean supernatural superpowers I didn't already possess? Are you inferring I already had supernatural superpowers?"

Hey, maybe with a shiny cape and a nice tiara, I could save the world!

"Alicia, what in the hell are you talking about?"

Alicia took another big gulp of coffee, and slipped her perfect feet into her dainty little heels. Jealously briefly reared its ugly head. I am genetically cursed with my father's feet. They are not pretty. I'm not proud of it, but I resent the hell out of those feet of hers. I might even consider giving up my heretofore unknown supernatural superpowers for feet like those. Just saying.

"Do you remember me mentioning Esmeralda was

a family name?" Alicia asked, referring to her previously referenced growing like a weed baby affectionately known as Esme.

"Yeah, I do," I replied. "Coincidentally, the same name runs in my family."

"Um, apparently not so much of a coincidence," Alicia replied, sinking her even white teeth into her lower lip. "After your little...experience, we did some digging. It seems you and I are descended from a common ancestor somewhere in the far distant past. On your mother's side."

"Are you trying to tell me I'm an SSI for real?" I gasped. I wished I had a mirror handy to see what complete and utter shock looked like. Then again, at close to three in the morning with no makeup and my tangled and dripping hair, perhaps it would be less traumatic to my already rattled senses if I didn't.

"Well, not exactly. It's a little more complicated than that," Alicia hedged. I *so* did not need complicated. After my little adventure in the afterlife, I'd actually managed to re-establish my relationships and learn to appreciate the important people in my life. I'd gained insight. I had a job. I had satisfying sex on a regular basis. Okay, so I still live over my father's garage, but I *like* it here. Doing fine now, thanks very much! Oh, sure, there were still days when I wished I could drive the karma bus, but overall? I did not need complicated. I did not want complicated. I do not do complicated. Don't ask, Max. Don't ask, don't ask, do *not* ask. Oh, who was I kidding? Of course, I would ask.

"Then what in the hell am I?"

"You, Maxine, are a Retriever." Alicia smiled as

though she'd said something extremely clever.

A *Retriever*? Seriously?

"Golden or Labrador?" I frowned.

"Oh, Max," Alicia tinkled gaily. "Always such a comedienne! But, seriously, a Retriever is a really rare and special being." A rare and special being? *Moi*? Well, finally! Someone interested in buying the swamp land I'd been selling for thirty-six years.

"Preaching to the choir, Alicia. So, okay I'm a Retriever, whatever that means. And not that it isn't nice to see you, but it would have been nicer, say around noon? What are you doing here at this hour?"

"A Retriever is one of the few beings who can move between realities, Max. It really is an extraordinary gift. We haven't had one in this region in years. Not since your mother," Alicia continued in a composed, dispassionate voice that should have been impossible considering the enormous bombshell she'd just dropped. My eyes, which at this hour were surely more red than blue, widened. I raised my brows so high into my dripping, disheveled hairline that I felt confident she'd never notice they needed a good waxing.

"My *mother*?" I barely recognized my own voice. It had never had that particular shrieking tone before. At least not that I could remember.

Alicia nodded. "Yes, Max, your mother. Like SSI's, Retrievers tend to run in families. Your mother must have known, or at least suspected, you had inherited her abilities. Our investigation shows that when she learned she had a terminal condition, she arranged to have your powers bound. You were so young, you see, and she knew she wouldn't be around to guide you. The records were sealed, and we had no idea until you crossed over during your, um, shall we say, unfortunate demise? Breaching the barrier between realities nullified the binding and poof! You showed up on the supernatural radar."

"The supernatural radar? I showed up on the supernatural radar?" I repeated blankly. "So what? Does someone sit around on a cloud somewhere watching little mystical blips twenty-four-seven?"

I rose from the sofa and made my way to the stainless steel sink and poured the remainder of my coffee down the drain. I wasn't sure how I knew it, but I sensed this new wrinkle in the fabric of my reality would require a drink with slightly more kick than my beloved java. Had my father known? I felt slightly betrayed but only for a heartbeat. I mean, realistically, even if he knew, what could he have done about it other than hope to hell my mother's binding held up? In zero to sixty I'd gone from feeling merely exhausted to feeling like I'd been sawed in half by a magician, punched in the gut by the heavyweight champion of the world, trampled by the bulls in Pamplona, and dumped in a ditch by the side of the road.

"Really, Max," Alicia said, moving to stand beside me and place her hand with its perfectly pink-tipped nails on my shoulder. "I know this is probably a bit of a shock, and you're upset now, but once you have some time to absorb it, you'll realize this is a great gift."

"Upset? Who's upset? I'm so freakin' thrilled I could fart glitter!" That's me, totally skilled at burying deep emotional issues under layers of sarcasm. Now *that's* a great gift! Why did people keep trying to push me outside the box? I like the box. It's my box. "Wait a minute! If I showed up on the radar after my death, why are you only telling me this now?"

For the first time in our limited acquaintance, Alicia looked profoundly uncomfortable. She tugged the cup from my unresisting fingers and rinsed both mine and hers in the sink. She planted them upside-down in the dish drainer on the counter, then twisted my threadbare dishtowel fretfully around her hands in an attempt to dry them.

"Well, we did suspect you might be somewhat resistant to the news. Perhaps I should tell you a little bit about what a Retriever actually *does*," she offered tensely. She stared over my shoulder and began to outline the benefits—i.e. duties—of a Retriever. I could tell she'd memorized it. Either that, or her supernatural superpowers gave her the ability to read from a paranormal teleprompter that had dropped from the sky somewhere behind my back.

"Well, as I told you already, a Retriever is a rare and special being. A Retriever can move between realities, meaning you can operate both here among the living, as well as on the other side."

"No offense, Alicia, but been-there-done-that. Why on Earth would I want to go back to the other side?" Frankly, I'd found the afterlife disappointing. I freely admit I'd bought into my Catechism teacher, Sister Mary Eloise's—better known among the Sunday school set as Sister Myrtle Elephant—hype. You know, pearly gates, angels on clouds, harp music, cute little cherubs zipping around scattering rose petals. The reality hadn't even come close. The afterlife I found resembled an abandoned bus station littered with empty cups and old newspapers with orange plastic chairs chained along the wall. And it reeked.

Apparently the celestial decorator aimed for a nice retro juvenile detention center look. Instead of pearly gates I found two stainless steel elevators glinting beneath garish arrows pointing north and south. The message on the arrows was written in some hieroglyphic language defying translation, but honestly, it didn't take a rocket scientist to figure it out. And the guardian of the gates? Well, Marvin Jenks would never be mistaken for anyone's idea of a benevolent St. Peter. And I said as much to Alicia.

"Oh, Maxine, really." She waved away my objections impatiently. "I told you before, that wasn't the pearly gates, it was the Office of Central Processing. It isn't anywhere, really. It's a bureaucratic sidebar and no one ever ends up there. Well, except you. I guess now we know why."

"We do?" She'd lost me. Not so surprising under the circumstances, I suppose, but I was usually a little quicker on the uptake. Must be a result of my current caffeine deficiency. Maybe I shouldn't have been so quick to dump my coffee down the sink. The fact I could so negligently waste my dark roasted ambrosia testified to my current state of mind.

Alicia sighed impatiently. "The binding? Threw off the natural order? Anyway, where was I? Oh, yes, a Retriever can move between realities. So for instance, if an inept trainee like your friend Buddy, causes a Death in Error as he did in your case, the soul would generally go to the Between, like everyone else's does, to be sorted out. A Retriever can go into the Between, find the soul, and return it to its body. Assuming the body has not yet been discovered and pronounced dead. If we'd known about you when Buddy caused the two erroneous deaths before yours, you conceivably could have gone in and brought those people back."

"So what you're telling me, Alicia, is I should be called a Fixer, not a Retriever. Basically, someone screws up and I fix it," I grumbled shortly. "You know what? I don't really think I'm interested in the position. I have a job now. Thanks anyway." I still worked part-time for my dad at Logan's Hardware, but since Roger and I were dating, I'd also started putting in a few days a week as his office manager. Just like old times. Except, well, now we were divorced.

"Well, here's the thing," Alicia stammered. "We have a bit of a situation."

"A situation?" I realized the only hope I had of getting something stronger than coffee at this point was to have a mental margarita. Since imaginary cocktails weren't as satisfying, I gave up and brewed another pot of java.

"Yes. At first it was just single, random unscheduled deaths here and there, easy to overlook. But the frequency has been increasing and this time it involved our region. As nearly as we can determine, your friend Buddy has gone rogue. He couldn't cut it as a Grim, so rather than admit defeat and take another position, it looks like he's chosen to align himself with the other side. And he's getting a bit more adventurous. His most recent stunt involved a small plane. You, Maxine, are the only hope we have," Alicia concluded fervently.

"First, let me go on record as saying that Buddy-the-Failed-Grim-Reaper-in-Training is no friend of mine. Second, if his orientation to his position resembled the one Marvin provided me for yours, no wonder the poor sod couldn't make a go of it. You guys really need to revamp your human resources department. Maybe come up with some kind of comprehensive divisional orientation or something. Third, this is not my problem and there isn't any reason I should make it my problem."

Alicia took a deep breath and let it out slowly. "Actually, Max, there *is* a reason you might want to consider making it your problem. Roger McCoy was on that plane."

Chapter Two

May I state for the record that Karma is one crazy bitch with a sick sense of humor? What did she have against me, anyway? Okay, there was that one questionable little period in college when I'd…um, yeah, never mind. Some things are never meant to be shared. And maybe before my erroneous death, I'd allowed myself to wallow in self-pity while I let my life go to hell in a hand-basket. Sure, it took death to show me what was important and what was a product of my own overactive insecurities, but as I may have stated before, I'm a reasonably intelligent woman. I'd learned my lesson. I had the inside track. It really is a wonderful life. No disrespect to the movie version. Couldn't they just leave me alone?

My hands shook, and I couldn't blame the caffeine. If Alicia was telling the truth—and honestly, why would she drop in at two in the morning to make this crap up—Roger was dead. Unless I agreed to become some kind of mystical bloodhound, he would stay that way. I didn't think a *cup* of coffee was nearly enough fortification for this news, so I grabbed the pot, rummaged in my catch-all silverware drawer, and scored a straw. Eureka! Most people might worry the scorching liquid would melt the plastic. I know better. From experience. Trust me, it works.

"Um, Max, do you really think that's a good idea?"

Alicia asked nervously as I continued to stare into space and greedily slurp the java straight from the pot, which was hardcore, even for a dedicated java junkie like me. "Maybe you should calm down until we talk this through."

Seriously? Have you ever noticed how the people who tell you to calm down are invariably the ones who riled you up in the first place? It would be nice if just once I could take a time out from being a grown-up. Deep down, I knew as soon as I wrapped my head around this, I would do it. Whatever *it* was. Of course I would do it. I mean, we were talking about Roger. He'd do the same thing for me. At least I think he would do the same thing for me. The guy was a giver. After all, he'd spent months in war-torn, third world countries targeted by terrorists to perform pro-bono surgeries on cute little orphans crawling with lice and heaven only knew what else. What was a little otherworldly snatch and grab compared to that?

Alicia continued to regard me with a worried expression, and I realized I was making that annoying sound you make when you get to the bottom of the glass and keep sucking on the straw. Yeah, that one. I reluctantly put the now empty coffee pot aside and took a deep breath. "What do I have to do?"

"So, you'll do it?" Alicia's glow amped up as though she'd been hit by a nuclear power surge. I wondered how her husband managed to ever get any sleep.

"We're talking about Roger, Alicia. Did you really have any doubt I'd agree?"

"Well, no…I knew you'd agree…eventually. But I had no idea how long it would take you to get around to it. We're on a tight schedule here. What time is it, anyway?" She tapped her wrist. *Why do people point at their wrist when they ask for the time? I don't grab my crotch when I ask for the restroom.*

"It's two forty five," I punctuated the announcement with a jaw cracking yawn. I wonder if it ever occurred to the paranormal employment division that even we rare and special beings function better on eight hours of sleep.

"Oh my stars!" Alicia cried out, jumping to her feet. "We've already lost nearly four hours. Hurry, Max, go get dressed. Where's your laptop?" I frowned down at my jeans and sweatshirt. I thought I was already dressed. I opened my mouth to point out the obvious, when Alicia spotted my laptop on the kitchen counter and made a bee-line. "Wear something nice, Max. You don't want to meet the Grim for the first time looking like a community college drop-out," Glow Girl tossed over her shoulder as she powered up the computer and pulled a flash drive and portable GPS from the bottom of a large canvas purse I hadn't even noticed she brought with her. Canvas in February? Honestly, even I knew better than that! Of course, I had Denise, the fashionista, to keep me on the seasonal straight and narrow.

Alicia wired the GPS up to my laptop and plugged the flash drive into the USB port. While she rat-tat-tat-tapped on the keyboard, I shuffled into my bedroom to change. Going on three in the morning with an outside temperature hovering somewhere around cold as a witch's boob in a brass bra was no time to contemplate style. Grim Reaper or not. In the end, my jeans and running shoes won out. My one concession to fashion was the new lapis lazuli colored cashmere turtleneck I'd purchased on my recent trip into retail hell with Denise. Roger said it matched my eyes.

Sadly, as expected, my hair had reached the point of no return. No way this side of the afterlife could I blow-dry the stubborn mess into the straighter style I preferred. I settled for painfully dragging a brush through the thick, tangled mass of curls until it settled into a full, dark cloud around my shoulders. Casual, yet elegant, that's me. Uh huh.

"Wear your mother's necklace, Maxine," Alicia called from the other room. Wear my mother's necklace? Was the SSI trying to sabotage what little degree of style I had? And how did Alicia even know about the necklace? Of course given the current situation and recent disclosures, I guess the only thing that should surprise me was that anything could still surprise me.

My mother's necklace was heavy and ornate. An elaborate, baroque-styled pendant with a huge cabochon in the center, ringed by smaller facet cut stones whose color coordination and arrangement had never made any sense to me. The entire hot mess dangled from a thick, twisted gold chain and weighed nearly as much as Sir Chicken Caesar. If you knew my cat personally, you would understand the significance. I suspected hanging it around my neck carried the risk of turning me into Quasimoto's younger and far more attractive sister. With the gold market at an all-time high, I could probably cash it in for enough to buy a new car. Still it had been my mother's, and I loved it from a purely sentimental standpoint. But honestly? It was not something I would ever wear. In a word?

Fugly!

I dug under the piles of white cotton Grammy pants in my underwear drawer and wrapped my fingers around the long, velvet case. I yanked it free, ignoring the jumbled mess I'd made of my questionable lingerie. It had been so long since I'd looked at the thing—at least twenty years—the box actually creaked when I opened it. I carefully withdrew and draped the heavy amulet around my neck, grimacing in the mirror at the way it detracted from the soft, woolen drape of the cashmere over my padded, push-up bra enhanced bosom.

Hey, some of us need all the help we can get, okay?

Sorry, Mom, I thought. I don't know what you saw in this thing, but it just isn't doing it for me. I stretched the turtleneck collar out far enough to drop the offending object inside my sweater and headed back to the living room. Alicia finished her work with my laptop, and dropped the flash drive into her out of season bag, turning to me as I re-entered the room.

"Where's the necklace?" she asked in a worried voice.

"Right here." I confidently patted my foundation garment lifted and separated girls.

"Just make sure you don't lose it. You'll need it," Alicia warned.

"It's fugly, Alicia. I'm sad to report my mother apparently had horrendous taste in accessories."

Alicia rolled her eyes and sighed. "No one ever intended it to be a fashion statement, Max. It's a piece designed strictly for power and protection. The stones were carefully chosen for just that purpose." She bit out each word slowly and carefully. When dealing with children, use small words and enunciate carefully, that's always been my motto. I guess Alicia heard how well that worked for me.

"Huh!" Queen of Eloquence, that's me! I tugged the offending jewel from the inside of my sweater and peered at it more carefully. Alicia strode briskly to where I stood and tugged the heavy piece from my curious fingers.

"The jade? Historically known for good luck. Also helps you to recognize yourself as a spiritual being, accept your surroundings for what they are, and instill a sense of detachment from chaos. More importantly, it assists the wearer in sensing truth in all situations." Alicia instructed in an impatient tone, pointing to each stone in turn. "Amber serves as a protection against taking on the pain of others. Citrine and amethyst transform and dispel negative energy. Aquamarine is a stone that imparts courage and strength." *Oh hell, I was pretty sure I would need more than one of those!*

"Smoky quartz facilitates the cooperation of multiple entities toward a common goal," she continued. "And the large quartz crystal in the center? That one stimulates psychic perceptions, reminds you that you are a spiritual being, and helps keep you receptive to higher guidance. If I understand the process correctly, the necklace will also get you in and out of the Between, and you need to understand how imperative it is you keep it with you at all times once you cross over."

So, let's see. My assignment, should I choose to accept it—and realistically I didn't have much of a choice if I wanted Roger back—was as follows: drive off into the night to an unknown destination following the directions of a mystically infused GPS, meet the Grim Reaper, cross over to the other side, locate Roger and any additional accidentally dead passengers, round everyone up and shuttle them back to the land of the living before their bodies were discovered on a snowy mountaintop in Colorado. The entire expedition courtesy of an enchanted necklace. Check. Sure. No problem. Was I the only one who strongly suspected we were all screwed?

"Got it," I replied with far more bravado than I felt.

"All righty then, let's get moving."

"Wait!" I had a thought. It happens occasionally. Caesar rubbed up against my ankles as if he would never see me again. And maybe he wouldn't. I couldn't just leave him on his own to miss me, starve, or claw the drapes to ribbons. I pulled out my cell phone and sent my sister a quick text saying I was going to meet Roger for a few days and asked her to feed the cat. My family loved Roger and hoped for a permanent reconciliation. I personally wasn't sure we were even close to that yet, but my family would be so thrilled at the thought we'd gone away together, they would never even think to question the quick getaway. Or the fact I'd informed them via text at three in the morning.

"Ready, now?" Alicia smiled, but she also tapped her toe in a manner denoting impatience. I nodded stiffly. Of course I wasn't ready, but I doubted I ever would be. Still, what choice did I have?

We clambered down the outside stairs to Roger's luxurious SUV which I'd offered to baby-sit during his absence. Sure, the gas mileage sucked, but something about barreling down the road in a big honking truck appealed to me. Alicia plugged in the GPS and pointed out the on-off button. I took a deep breath, and inserted the key in the ignition.

"Just follow the route I've programmed for you. It will take you right to the Grim Reaper. Morgan's a bit…intimidating, but underneath he's really a good guy. He'll explain how you cross over and provide you with all of the last minute directions you'll need for a successful retrieval," Alicia directed, then gave me a brief hug. She didn't share the details of what the consequences of an *unsuccessful* retrieval might be, and frankly, I couldn't bring myself to ask.

My little excursion into the unknown started out promisingly enough. I wiggled the mirrors into position and found to my delight those handy dandy electric seat warmers really do work. Before I'd even shifted into reverse and backed out of the drive, my butt was pretty much smoking hot. Ready for anything, I hit the button and turned on the GPS. It dinged, it donged, it did everything except play the Billboard top 100, and then a pleasant enough Stepford Wife's disembodied voice informed me my route had been mapped. She sounded helpful and trustworthy. *You think you're the first one to accuse me of being gullible? Don't judge me.* She and I navigated out of town with nary a problem, and I dared to hope for clear sailing. I barreled along, racing against the waning moon and the approaching snow. About twenty-five miles into the drive, the sky remained black, but the road had turned totally white. I suspected I might be in trouble. Still, I'm a glass half-full kind of girl. Mostly. I was driving a reliable vehicle on a fairly well-traveled road. What could go possibly go wrong? The thought had no sooner occurred to me when my mechanical guide interrupted to announce traffic appeared to be at a standstill somewhere ahead. An accident, maybe? Given the rapidly deteriorating road conditions, I wouldn't be surprised. She magnanimously offered to recalculate. Feeling my faith in the well-modulated voice was, thus far, well placed, I proceeded to exit the highway when my electronic traveling companion indicated I should do so. Oddly, I didn't notice any signs, but I figured she probably had the advantage of a satellite view, whereas I squinted ineffectually through a curtain of wind-whipped snow. Of course, it was probably a testament to my sanity that I considered anything odd at this stage. I decided it might be a good idea to mute the dulcet tones of the radio for the time being so I wouldn't miss a single thing my helpful female friend in the box had to say—until I found my way back onto a main road. I drove for less than a mile, both the visibility and the road conditions deteriorating by the minute, when my electronic traveling companion helpfully announced my destination loomed only a mile ahead. She'd found a shortcut! Hot damn!

The world is a cruel place. Especially an hour and a half into what should have been a one hour drive on a still dark February morning with a snow squall kicking up. At least the weatherman predicted a snow squall. Frankly, it looked more like an impending blizzard to me. Visibility had been reduced to nil, but since I found myself in the middle of nowhere, I took comfort in the fact at least there were no other cars on the road to worry about. I confidently sat behind the wheel of Roger's SUV with a mystically programmed GPS. I'd be fine. Who knew adverse weather conditions coupled with roads that had never even been included on a map, let alone programmed into a satellite, could render that delightful little piece of state of the art technology virtually useless? Yeah. This new road had no markers, no utility poles, basically no signs of life. It simply appeared to be a slash in the forest that should have been pavement, surrounded on both sides by trees linking their bare elbows together while bowing politely toward one another under a heavy blanket of snow. Apparently, the Grim Reaper lived in Antarctica.

I wrestled with the wheel in order to stay in the middle of the snow tree arch since it didn't appear that a plow, or any other vehicle, had preceded me. It was virtually impossible to tell where the road ended and the shoulder began. My faith in the GPS chick waned, though I had to admit even she couldn't have predicted the startled doe that decided to crash through the encroaching forest and bound directly into the path of my borrowed vehicle.

I'm a Pennsylvania girl, I know snow. I remained calm and shifted into neutral. I pumped the brakes and steered into the skid. In short, I did everything but stand on my head and spit wooden nickels. Happily, I managed to avoid broad-siding the frightened animal, who escaped into the forest with a graceful leap. Yay, me! Although the ungrateful wench didn't even spare me a backward glance, at least I wouldn't have to explain gory deer guts in the grill to Roger. Unfortunately, I *would* have to expound upon the crushed right fender, shattered headlight, and pleated hood. The damage stemmed from my successful deer avoidance maneuver and subsequent uncontrolled skid into an up close and personal embrace with a large, unforgiving tree. My honey would not be happy. Of course, first I had to successfully retrieve him. Otherwise, his reaction to a probable increase in his car insurance premium was a moot point. I swore I heard the electronic bitch laugh.

The Bitch-in-a-Box offered to recalculate. Yeah, like that would help. Convinced she'd now resorted to taunting me, I enjoyed a brief moment of empowerment when I flicked her switch off. Who needed her anyway? We both knew I was lost. And stuck. However, I wasn't immediately concerned. I'd topped off the gas tank before merging onto the interstate, and I knew my best bet was to crack a window, leave the engine running for heat, and wait for the auto club to arrive and tow me to the nearest garage. My splendid plan quickly bit the dust when I pulled out my cell phone and discovered this winter wonderland was a dead zone.

Well, wasn't that wucking fonderful?

Maybe I could somehow back up onto the road? Given the current weather conditions, the missing headlight might prove challenging, but progress is progress and I'd take what I could get. I slammed the lever into four-wheel drive, and jammed the gearshift into reverse. The tires whined on the ice slicked snow with a frustration which nearly matched my own— while the beam of the single remaining headlight cavorted in a crazy dance through the darkened rows of snow-frosted firs. I slammed the unenthusiastic transmission back and forth, repeatedly, grinding the protesting gears, in an attempt to muscle my way out.

Did I mention I'm from Pennsylvania and know snow? Yeah. Apparently knowing it and extricating oneself from it are two entirely different things."

After ten minutes I reluctantly admitted defeat. No

amount of rocking the heavy duty SUV would get me free. Not without some equally heavy duty chains, a tow truck, and maybe a couple of really jacked twenty-something guys with eight-pack abs and tight jeans. At least that's what I figured. At any rate watching them work might provide some entertainment as I slowly froze to death. I reclined the seat, rewarded my failed but heartfelt efforts with a swig of bottled water, and considered my options. My cell phone had no signal. My survival supplies consisted of one bottle of water and, if I was lucky, a couple of sticks of sugar free gum turning to stone in the bottom of my purse. I had no idea of my location, and no idea if, or when, another car might happen along. Adding to my misery was the certain knowledge my already limited time to reach the Grim Reaper and save Roger was slipping away.

Wait! Hadn't Box Bitch announced my destination was one mile ahead? And hadn't she offered that little pearl of wisdom about a half mile before I avoided the deer, became close personal friends with a tree, and decided it was time for her to shut up? Could civilization possibly be waiting with open arms less than three thousand feet away? Common sense told me to stay put. I was warm, uninjured, and safely locked inside my two ton steel box. Common sense, however, is not as common as you might think. Especially in my case. Except for the small area illuminated by my one sad headlight, the darkness pressed in on me from all sides. Although I'd never been subject to the malady before, I felt kind of claustrophobic. Besides I had a deadline to consider.

Having failed to pre-plan for an Arctic expedition, I doubted my cashmere sweater and little plaid, quilted vest were going to cut it. The vest wasn't very thick, but at least it added an additional layer. Layers were good, right? In addition, I'd had the unexpected foresight to wear a long, wool coat. I'd also stuffed gloves in my pocket, and draped a rather thin and loosely woven, but fully functional scarf around my neck. No, I didn't have a hat. I never wear a hat, no matter how cold it gets. In fact, I don't think I own one. I suspect it's a belated, subconscious form of childhood rebellion.

When we were kids, Stepmother Gail insisted on slapping a hat on my sister and me every day as soon as the temperature dropped below fifty degrees. She convincingly preached half of a person's body heat is lost through the top of their head. Since everyone knows heat rises, this always seemed to make perfect sense. My dark brown hair is thick and wavy and has a mind of its own. Consequently, for years I suffered the tragic malady of hat head, and endured the underestimated dangers of static electricity.

As an adolescent, I discovered this popular theory is nothing more than a myth inspired by a flawed interpretation of a vaguely scientific experiment conducted by the United States military. Sometime in the nineteen-fifties, a bunch of misguided but well-meaning volunteers were bundled in Arctic survival suits, and then exposed to bitterly cold conditions. Their heads were the only part of their bodies left uncovered, so no surprise they lost most of their body heat through their heads. Duh! If they'd been dressed in nothing except knee socks and hooded parkas, no doubt the heat loss from their backsides would have been just as statistically significant. Not that I am advocating anyone expose their buttocks to the elements in an attempt to prove my hypothesis. But, I digress. Admittedly, regardless of the facts, wrapping one's head, neck, and chest in layers of protection did always seem to *feel* warmer, and under the circumstances, it probably couldn't hurt to adhere to Gail's erroneous, but well intentioned advice.

I scrambled awkwardly over the seats to peruse the storage area under the deck in the back. Roger had been skiing in the Poconos with some colleagues last weekend, and knowing how religiously he adhered to the Procrastinator's Bible, I guessed he hadn't bothered to bring anything into the house when he'd returned. I grabbed the handle and tugged up the carpeted flap. Bingo! His black duffle bag was still there, the one that cost nearly as much as my car. I made a mental note to talk to him about renegotiating my alimony.

I pulled off my running shoes and tugged two pairs of heavy ski socks over my own thinner ones, yanking the second pair up over the hem of my jeans. It was a struggle to get the shoes back on, and far from comfortable, but it was definitely more practical. Of course, if I'd taken practicality into consideration, I would have worn *mukluks*. Who knew? Next, I donned a thick, ivory Aran sweater that smelled of Roger and made my heart beat painfully fast as it reminded me of what was at stake. I wrapped my scarf around my head and neck like a *hijab*, crossed the ends over my chest, and forced my black, wool coat over everything. The buttons strained heroically, and I felt like the kid from that Christmas movie who was so bundled up his arms stuck out from his body at a ninety degree angle no matter what he did. I imagined my current look was similarly attractive.

I spied a couple of granola bars of indeterminate age in the bottom of Roger's bag, and shoved them into my purse, along with my bottled water and the flashlight I'd retrieved from the glove box. I slung the strap across my body and took a deep breath. I didn't relish the thought of slogging through the snow in the dark, but if there was a chance I could still find the Grim Reaper and save the day, I had to take it. I decided to stick to the road, walk for a while, and if I didn't see any signs of life, hike back to the vehicle and hunker down until someone found me.

I took another deep breath, clicked off the ignition and climbed out. I closed the door, pressed the lock button on the key-fob, and dropped the keys into my coat pocket. The headlights, or rather headlight—singular—was on a timer and would stay on for a few minutes, so I set off at a relatively brisk clip in the direction I had been driving before my enviable deer avoidance skills put the kibosh to my forward motion.

I kept to the middle of the road, and somehow managed to remain mostly upright on the slick surface. Once I was out in the open and away from the vehicle, I realized it wasn't nearly as dark as I expected. The watery moonlight glowed over the endless blanket of white and reflected back an ethereal glow bright enough to make the flashlight redundant. The hushed winter scene really was quite beautiful, though frankly my anxiety precluded my ability to fully appreciate it as much as I might have under less stressful circumstances.

My breath rolled out in frosty little puffs, and I pulled my scarf up over my face as my nose hairs turned into icicles. The only sound I heard for a long while was the crunch of my feet in the crusty snow, and the labored rasp of my own breathing. My stomach churned. I decided it was due to neglecting my rather healthy appetite and not the anxiety I firmly suppressed. I convinced myself any noises I heard were tree limbs giving way under the weight of the snow. When I finally got home, I vowed to investigate a job as a weather bunny. Apparently it required no skill or accuracy whatsoever.

Did I mention this was supposed to be a squall?

After twenty minutes of brisk walking, combined with awkward sliding, and a few ungainly tripping episodes, I'd worked up quite a sweat—despite the cold. I could actually feel the moisture trickling down my back, between my breasts, and chafing against the armpits of my sweater. My knees were wet and ice encrusted where I'd landed on them at least twice. I stopped and looked around, squinting against the wind whipped snow stinging like icy needles against my exposed face. I knew I must have walked at least a mile, if not more. Yet, I saw nothing but bare, snow covered trees, and a long stretch of endless road. Not a house, not a light, not a hint of smoke curling from a chimney somewhere off in the distance. Nothing. A pretty Christmas card scene, but not necessarily a place I wanted to be. The GPS's, if you could call it that, calculations had obviously been wrong. Why was I not surprised?

I briefly debated the merit of soldiering on, and then decided my best course of action was to return to the relative safety of the SUV. As soon as I stopped moving, I felt the deadly cold seeping into my body.

The exertion that kept me warm while trekking along now worked against me as my exercise heated skin and wet clothes conspired to disperse my limited body heat into the frigid night air. I refused to panic. I knew my abandoned vehicle would have cooled down by now, but there was an automatic starter on the key fob and once the engine was re-started, it should heat up quickly.

Roger did love his luxuries, and at this point, his self-indulgence worked for me. I didn't know if the signal would engage from this distance, but I figured I could just keep hitting the button periodically as I slogged my way back, and at some point it should kick in and provide me with a toasty reception.

The snow fell hard enough to obliterate my footprints, making me glad I'd decided to stick to the road. At least finding my way back wouldn't be a problem. I pulled off my snow encrusted glove, and dug in my coat pocket for the keys. My stomach rose into my throat and threatened to choke me as I pulled off my second glove, and frantically dug in the other pocket. Then I proceeded to grope my way through every pocket in my jeans, and every compartment, pouch, and nether region of my purse. My heart pounded in earnest, and I shivered, and not only because of the cold. The keys were nowhere to be found. Maybe now was the time to panic?

I pulled the flashlight from my bag and shone it carefully back in the direction I'd traveled. I could barely see my own footprints for more than ten feet, never mind a set of keys. I could have lost them anywhere along the way. They could even be back near the vehicle. But what if I walked all the way back and they weren't? I began to dig around in the snow near my feet hoping they'd simply fallen out when I reached into my pocket for them. My hands and feet ached with the cold, but I ignored the pain and kept burrowing. Without those keys, I was totally screwed. The clammy chill that started when I ceased walking settled into my core. I trembled violently. With a doctor for an ex-husband, I knew this full body, teeth-chattering shivering was my body's attempt to generate additional heat, which probably meant I was no longer successfully maintaining mine. It had been a mistake to leave the SUV, I knew that now. But knowing didn't solve my problem. Hindsight is always better than looking in a mirror, right? Yeah, story of my life.

With a return to the vehicle out of the equation, my only option seemed to be to keep moving forward. At least I thought it was my only option. My mind felt sluggish and cloudy and it seemed like too much trouble to process a complete thought. I had a fleeting epiphany this was probably not the best news.

The cold-stiffened muscles of my legs screamed in protest with every step. My knees had to be persuaded to bend, and my gait had the ataxic grace of a zombie. I forced myself to put one foot in front of the other, and eventually drifted closer to the side of the road, vaguely recognizing if a car actually did come along, I was probably physically unable to get out of the way in a hurry. I never noticed the lump in the snow. Of course, doing the monster mash shuffle, I couldn't have lifted my leg high enough to avoid it anyway. A jolt of white hot agony shot through my ankle as I tripped and went flying into the ditch. Mercifully, most of me was too numb to feel the pain. The blood dripping into my eye was my first clue I'd apparently hit my head. What the hell! A cracked skull already killed me once. Was it too much to hope for a little variety? Oh, that's right. The busted noggin' wouldn't do me in. This time I would simply freeze to death.

Moving required too much exertion. Snow packed the neck of my sweater, and rivulets of melting water trickled down, seeping into my already damp clothes. I finally determined I had to make an attempt. First I struggled to sit, and then powered myself upright. I immediately collapsed with a whole lot less effort than it had taken me to rise. Right about now I was ready to punch Jack Frost in the snowballs.

I checked my watch. Four-thirty. Maybe just a short rest. I laid back in the snow, only half aware it was a mistake. My ears burned with the fire of a thousand suns, and I absently realized my scarf had fallen down from my head. I struggled to pull it up, succeeding minimally. That little activity exhausted me. I thought of saunas, greenhouses, coffee…anything warm and soothing. The only sound in the world was the thud of my blood pumping in my ears. Suddenly, I had an overwhelming urge to pee. Figures. I turned my head from side to side squinting through the darkness. Nope, not a port-a-potty in sight. Just my luck.

Hours later—or maybe it was minutes—I squinted at my watch again. The numbers blurred. Despite the sub-freezing temperature and semi-blizzard conditions, heat crawled up my neck and scorched my cheeks with suffocating warmth. My numb fingers fumbled with my coat buttons. I dragged my scarf away from my head and neck. But, as soon as the air hit me, the illusion of warmth dissipated leaving only snow, cold, and darkness. Now I'd pulled off half of my clothes, and had no energy to rectify the situation. Out of the corner of my eye, I detected movement.

A dark shape slinked out of the trees on my left. Hooray, I'm saved! Praying the shadowy figure was human, I struggled to identify it. As it moved closer, its glowing, preternaturally green eyes locked onto mine. Small, frosty puffs of breath huffed from its nose and mouth. A mouth filled with large, pointed teeth, teeth gleaming as though they might mean business. Wolf! An enormous black wolf.

I had a fleeting thought I should be afraid, but the fear seemed to be floating somewhere outside of my immediate circle. It was way too much trouble to chase it down and bring it back. I was so tired. A tear squeezed from the corner of my eye and ran into my hair where it froze almost at once. *I'm sorry, Roger*, I whispered, in case he could hear me wherever he was. I briefly wondered if my body was numb enough to dull the pain when the beast ripped my throat out. I heard a pathetic whimpering sound, then realized it came from me. Hot breath heated my face. A cold, wet nose curiously nudged my cheek, followed by the lick of a warm, rough tongue. I reached up to bury my hand in the thick, warm, coat and waited for death. *Nice doggy.*

Chapter Three

My next semi-coherent thought was that I actually *had* died this time. And gone straight to Hell. I opened one eye and found myself in a strange room enveloped in shadows lit only by a blazing fireplace. Logically I knew on some level the burning pain wracking my extremities resulted from my returning blood flow now that I was indoors and swaddled like a papoose in heavy quilts. I forced the other eye open and observed a man, his back to me, squatting in front of the fire adding wood. As he rose to his feet, I gasped at his size. Well over six feet with massively broad shoulders that strained the seams of his flannel shirt and tapered to a narrow waist. His high, tight butt deliciously filled out the worn denim of his jeans. Even in my pain wracked semi-stupor, I could appreciate the view. A great ass is a great ass. I must have made an inadvertent sound because the man turned his head slightly to glance over his shoulder in my direction. His long, dark hair obscured my view of his face.

"How do you feel?" His voice, as deep and smooth as melted chocolate, seemed to permeate my entire being and flowed through my bones. I grew warmer by the second.

"I'm not sure…" I croaked, surprised at the fractured hoarseness of my own voice. I tried to smile, but my cracked lips refused to cooperate. My wind bitten cheeks stung with the effort. "Thank you for finding me. How did you? Find me, I mean?"

"I was expecting you. When you didn't arrive as scheduled, I went out to have a look around." He picked up a mug from the mantel and moved toward me with a slow and dangerous grace that set a flock of butterflies loose in my stomach. His hair still fell across his face like a dark curtain, and I could barely make out anything except one brilliant green eye and the chiseled ridge of one high cheekbone.

"You…you're the Grim Reaper? Somehow I'd pictured someone a little more skeletal wearing black robes and maybe twirling a sickle."

"I'm Morgan Kane, yes. You look like hell." I bristled at the smile in his voice. I didn't doubt he was right, but still, I didn't think it was very polite of him to point it out.

"Good of you to notice. I can now check that off my bucket list," I snapped back testily.

He didn't respond. Instead he slid a flannel encased arm beneath my shoulders and held the mug to my lips. He smelled of wood smoke and pine and something more subtle and slightly sweet. I'll admit, I found it very appealing.

"Here, drink this." He shoved the mug under my nose, which all but eliminated any hint of his alluring aroma. The concoction reeked.

"What is it?" I took a sniff. *Ewww.*

"Just some herbal tea with probably more sugar than you'll like, but you need it."

"I realize I probably owe you my life, and I hate to seem like an ingrate, but I really have kind of an aversion to tea."

Truth be known, I was a bit of an Anglophile. I had read everything Jane Austen had ever written, voraciously followed the antics of the British Royal family, and considered Colin Firth the greatest actor of all time. I loved the *idea* of tea. Especially when it also involved dainty little sandwiches, scones, and assorted cakes. Lots and lots of cakes. But no matter how many times I tried, I could not acclimate myself to the *taste* of tea. Espresso ran in my veins. I was on a first name basis with Juan Valdez and his burro.

"Any chance you have coffee?" I worked to free my arms from the cocoon of blankets. "Here, let me up, you don't have to wait on me."

He tilted the cup toward my mouth. "Drink it. Of course I have coffee, but you aren't having any right now. Caffeine is a vasoconstrictor and that's the last thing you need. Maybe later. You need to get warmed up from the inside, and your body can use the sugar for energy, so drink this." He tipped the cup until I had no choice but to swallow or drown. "And stop squirming. You need to stay still for a while until your body re-warms. You move around too much and all of the cold blood rushes from your extremities to your heart...you don't want to risk an irregular heartbeat, lady. We've already wasted more time than we can afford."

Kane propped a couple of pillows behind me and retreated back into the shadows. I brought the mug to my dry lips and choked down a few more sips—trying really hard to be cooperative so we could get this dog and pony show on the road. It was then I realized my arms were completely bare. Gripping the handle of the mug tightly in one hand, I used the other to perform a quick, but relatively thorough inventory under the quilts. My nudity extended well beyond my upper extremities. My shocked gasp must have alerted him to my discovery because the one side of his mouth I could discern in the fire-lit darkness quirked up in a grin.

"Who, um…I mean where are my…"

"You were soaking wet and had managed to urinate all over yourself." His words were matter-of-fact, but his tone was amused no matter how he tried to hide it. Truthfully, I didn't get the impression he was trying very hard. "I washed your clothes. They should be dry in another ten minutes or so."

"I *urinated* all over my…? And you…? Oh. My. God."

What little body heat I had managed to re-acquire was quickly diverted into my face in a fiery rush. After working for years in Roger's office, I was no prude when it came to bodily functions or nudity in general. Well, as long as it was clinically related and someone else's nudity. Wait a minute? He washed my cashmere sweater? Damn! My beautiful new sweater was toast. I knew it. In fact, I probably could give it to one of my pre-pubescent nieces by the time it came out of the dryer. Again, I digress. However, mourning the loss of my sweater was preferable to concentrating on the fact that I was naked in some remote cabin with a perfect stranger who also happened to be the Grim Reaper. A very hot Grim Reaper who had thoughtfully stripped off and laundered my pee-soaked panties. Charming! Who says I don't know how to make a memorable first impression?

"Would it make you feel any better if I said I was a doctor?" he asked trying for solemnity but failing miserably.

"No…" I burrowed as far down into my makeshift cocoon as I was able. "I don't know…maybe. Are you?"

"No," he chuckled, sending the heat rushing back into my cheeks. Well, at least they'd been *nice* panties. Another Gail-ism instilled in me until it may as well have been tattooed into my brain—never leave the house wearing ratty undies in case you get into an accident. Gail was turning out to be quite the underappreciated genius.

"Look, there's no reason to get all worked up. It's the body's natural reaction to hypothermia. The vessels in the extremities constrict and force the fluid to the core to conserve heat. The kidneys start working overtime to process the fluid…it's gotta go somewhere, right?"

I kept my eyes averted while I choked down another big gulp of the vile tasting liquid, hoping it might dislodge the thick lump of mortification stuck in my throat. The subsequent sips weren't as distasteful as the first, but they did nothing to alleviate my embarrassment.

"Do you, ah…" I cleared my throat harshly. "Do you have something I could, um, put on until my clothes are dry?" I risked a glance from under my lashes as I heard him approach. My libido meter escalated off the charts when I realized he was unbuttoning his shirt and peeling it from his wide shoulders and smooth, broad chest. Hardly daring to breathe, I averted my eyes, refusing to look, until a flannel filled fist was held right under my nose. Well, okay, maybe I peeked a *little*.

Like you wouldn't? I am a woman. I've been

divorced for over two years, and though my ex and I are currently dating, a shattered relationship isn't rebuilt overnight, and my hormones are not in hibernation. So I looked. More than once. I admit it. Satisfied?

"Here, put this on. It's warm already."

With the mug in one hand, and the other clutching a quilt to my bare chest, I didn't have a hand free to accept the proffered shirt. He noticed my dilemma and pried the mug from my stiff fingers. Setting it on a small table next to the sofa, he held the shirt allowing me to slip it on one arm at a time without relinquishing my grip on the blankets. He turned his back and walked over to the fireplace to poke at the flaming logs, giving me a measure of privacy while I fumbled with the buttons. Buttoning a shirt is not the easiest task in the world with fingers still half frozen and as nimble as breakfast sausages. Hot as Hades and a gentleman, too? Go figure. Then again, it wasn't like he hadn't already seen everything I owned. I buried my nose in a fistful of the fabric as the singular scent of the man rose from the warm folds of his shirt. Drawing in a deep breath, I detected the mingled aromas of pine and wood smoke, a hint of men's cologne, and…yes, jelly doughnuts. Don't get me wrong, I like pine and wood smoke and cologne, though a lot of them are a little too strong for my taste. I am, however, a complete sucker for jelly doughnuts. The unusual fragrance combination incited my body to produce heat in areas that shouldn't really be a priority at the moment. I shook my head to rid myself of the inappropriate thoughts. So maybe he was built like the hero in a fantasy I wasn't even aware I had, and maybe he had saved my life, but he was a complete stranger. I had a steady guy. Roger! Oh, yeah...the reason I was here in the first place!

Hey, can't blame a recently hypothermic naked girl if her thoughts are a little scattered, right?

"So," I began in a shaky voice. "What's next?"

He tossed another log into the grate—causing an explosion of glowing embers to erupt and scatter on the hearth. The flames burst into life illuminating the rich bronze of his torso and the long lines of thick, angry scars running along the right side of his body from his armpit, along his ribcage, and into the waistband of his jeans near the small of his back. They appeared to be claw marks, like something had caught him from behind and dragged at him. He stepped back from the light quickly when I gasped.

"Did your wolf do that?" I breathed nervously. The wounds certainly looked like they'd been inflicted by an animal. A large and unfriendly animal.

"My wolf?" He laughed quietly but without mirth. "No, my wolf didn't do this."

"Then what hap...I'm sorry." By now you may have noticed I am not typically at a loss for words. However, at this point, I was tripping over my own tongue and actually stammered. "It's really none of my business."

"You're right, it *is* none of your business, but since I played ladies' maid with your panties, very nice panties by the way, I suppose that entitles you to a personal question or two."

If he intended to distract me by reminding me of my humiliating loss of bodily fluids, he succeeded. I dropped the subject and took another big gulp of the revolting tea. He poked ferociously at the logs with a hooked iron pole, shifting them into a position that would keep them burning for a while.

"Finish your tea. There's a bathroom through there," he began in a husky voice, jerking his chin toward a hallway to the left of the fireplace. "The kitchen is through here." He indicated the doorway on the other side. "I'll leave your clothes outside the bathroom. Come out to the kitchen as soon as you're ready. We need to get moving." And then he was gone.

I quickly swung my bare legs over the side of the sofa, tugging at the hem of the flannel shirt to cover my assets as best I could, and pushed up from the deep sofa cushions. My ankle immediately protested the attempt to bear weight, and let me know in no uncertain terms it wasn't happy. I dropped back to the sofa with a sharp yelp, sucking my breath in through my teeth with a pained hiss. I stuck my bare leg out in front of me and grimaced. I had been too cold and out of it to pay much attention before, but my ankle looked like rising bread dough in a hot oven, and sported an impressive kaleidoscope of colors. Some supernatural superhero I turned out to be. I could barely take care of myself and they were entrusting me with the lives of others?

Can we say suckers, boys and girls?

Morgan Kane must have heard my piercing squeal, and came pounding into the room. He stopped inside the doorway, panting as though he'd run a mile. Maybe he had. What did I know about Grim Reapers and their activities? Well, aside from the obvious one. His face settled into an odd expression when he saw me wearing nothing but his shirt and my necklace, with one bare leg sticking out in front of me.

"What's wrong?" he huffed.

"It's my ankle," I caught my lip in my teeth and hissed when I probed a particularly tender spot. "I guess I turned it when I fell. I don't think anything's broken, but it sure hurts like hell. I hope you have an elastic bandage or something or I'm going to have a problem."

I glanced up and offered him a wry grin. My eyes widened, and the grin slowly faded. I sat back slowly and carefully against the cushions. The room had lightened now, and he'd pulled back his hair into a thick ponytail leaving his face open and exposed to inspection. His left eye drooped a bit, and his mouth on that side froze in a perpetual frown where a laceration had skirted too close to his lips and tugged them down as it scarred. His cheek bore thick, white ropes of raised tissue curving down and back beneath his long, dark hair toward his ear and neck. From a purely clinical perspective, it looked as though the gashes had never even been sutured, just simply left to heal while splayed open along his face. The right side of his face was untouched, and so heartbreakingly beautiful it only compounded the tragedy of the left's horrible disfigurement.

I was momentarily distracted from the scars by the smooth, bronzed width of his chest and shoulders, and the butterflies in my stomach that started up the moment he appeared in the doorway. He watched me intently. When I'd asked him about the scars on his trunk earlier, he didn't seem all that open to discussion. Oh well, so maybe I should just ignore the elephant in the room and see how that worked out.

"Can you, uh…help me to the bathroom?"

"Huh?" His mouth dropped open. I guess he'd expected a little more reaction. Fear, horror, shrinking away in terror? I doubted it would be the first time it had happened. Maybe that's why he lived in such an isolated spot? None of my business. I needed him to help me save Roger. That was the one and only reason I was here. I didn't need to know his life story to do it.

"The bathroom...you know, it's morning...nature calls...injured ankle," I recited tolerantly, if a little self-consciously. "Could you please help me get in there? I hate to ask, I mean, at this point, I realize you may be more familiar with my excretory functions than any other man I know, and probably way more familiar than you want to be, but I don't seem to be able to fly solo at the moment."

"Oh, uh." He started toward me, as if roused from a stupor. "Sure...no problem. By the way, do you usually wear glasses?"

"Only for reading, why?" He stopped halfway across the room.

"Just wondered."

"I noticed your face if that's why you're asking." My lips peeled back in an evil grin. I freely admit it, I'm really not very good at ignoring elephants. *Don't pretend this surprises you*

"Oh." He simply stared at me as if he expected me to elaborate. I didn't. Finally I cleared my throat when he continued to stand there.

"Um, bladder capacity of a lima bean over here...could you give a girl a hand?" He finally closed the distance between us and easily scooped me up as though I was one of those thin and wispy girls I like to imagine I am. He carried me to the bathroom door and then stood there looking down at me with a puzzled expression.

"S'cuse me." I rested patiently in his arms while he stared. I wondered if he'd suffered some kind of concurrent brain injury when he acquired the scars. He seemed to become rather easily distracted. Maybe he had focal seizures? Perhaps I should carry something shiny to capture his attention? "This would probably be a lot simpler if you put me down."

He seemed startled to realize he still held me and lowered me too quickly. I grabbed at his shoulder for balance at exactly the same instant as he leaned down to steady me. My hand clutched at his collar on the left side of his neck, right below the ragged remains of what had once been his ear.

"Jaysus!" I hissed through clenched teeth. I tugged his hair back and tried to get a better look, even as he tried to straighten away from me. I lightly traced my fingertips down the path of his scars along his cheek, coming to rest on the bony ridge of his jaw. What had the bastard who treated him used for sutures, shoelaces? "I hope you sued the sonofabitch."

"Excuse me?"

"The doctor who sewed you up. He must have gotten his license in a box of cereal."

He blinked in confusion at my indignation. I bet he'd expected me to be frightened, or horrified, or disgusted. I was none of those things. I was incensed and downright pissed on his behalf. Morgan Kane, the Grim Reaper, reached up and gently tugged my fingers away from his face. I looked everywhere but at him, fidgeting uncomfortably.

"I, uh…I'm sorry. I had no right to say that. It's only…well, I'm sorry, okay?" There was some deep emotion swirling in his haunted green eyes I couldn't readily identify. My heart stuttered, and my breath caught in my throat. I hadn't meant to sound so harsh. I bet he dealt with people's cruelty all the time. Although to be honest, he looked like the kind of man who could give as good as he got. It didn't often happen, but for once I wished I could take my words back. Sometimes I have this tiny little problem inserting a filter between my thoughts and my mouth.

I know, it shocks me, too.

"Well, then…I'll just get your things and leave them here outside the door. There should be an extra toothbrush in the cabinet if you need it. Can you manage?" he asked, ignoring my attempt at an apology and turning me toward the bathroom.

"A toothbrush would be great." Maybe it would scrub the taste of the damn tea out of my mouth. I expelled a sigh of relief he'd chosen to overlook my awkward outburst. I mean, the guy *was* the Grim Reaper after all. It probably was in my best interest to play nice. And whether I could manage or not didn't signify. He'd already washed my undies. I really preferred to wipe my own butt, thanks. "And that elastic bandage if you have one. I'm guessing I'll need it to be able to walk?"

"Sweetheart, I have a strong hunch you'll not only need to be able to walk, you'll need to be able to run." And with that cryptic remark, he pulled the bathroom door closed and left me alone.

Chapter Four

After awkwardly taking care of business, washing my hands, and splashing my face, I found the extra toothbrush exactly where the Grim Reaper said it would be. Fortunately, he'd also left one of those little sample sized tubes of toothpaste. I should probably think about doing something similar in my powder room in case I ever have unexpected guests who needed to perform personal hygiene.

What? It could happen.

I removed the toothbrush from its cellophane wrapper, and on my third attempt my stiffened fingers managed to actually get the toothpaste on the brush and into my mouth. Have you ever noticed how hard it is to keep toothpaste on your toothbrush but once it hits the sink it sticks like super glue? Just saying. The minty freshness burned like a blowtorch on my dry, cracked lips, but I did feel slightly more human after I'd scrubbed and rinsed.

I opened the door a crack and snatched my clothes. I was nearly beside myself with joy to find my underthings, tucked in among the pile the Grim Reaper had deposited outside of the bathroom, had survived unscathed. Otherwise I would have been forced to go uncomfortably commando—since there was no way in hell I was climbing into panties of unknown origin even if they had been offered. Starting with the elastic bandage Kane had left on top of the pile, I did a passable figure eight wrap on my ankle. It felt better almost immediately. I donned my pink lace bra and then carefully threaded my swathed ankle through one leg of the matching panties while balanced precariously on my other foot. Finally I tugged them up, smoothing them over my hips. They really were nice panties, made my tummy appear flatter than it actually was, and hugged my generously rounded bottom to perfection.

Thank God I'd worn a pretty pair of matching scanties and not the serviceable white cotton Grammy pants I favored on an everyday basis. Cotton and incontinence. I would have never been able to face Morgan Kane again. He might secretly think I was a complete dipwad, but he had to admire my taste in lingerie.

Of course, Roger was my guy, but since the Grim Reaper's first impression of me had already been less than stellar, I'd grab what perks I could find. Sadly, as I'd feared, my lovely blue cashmere sweater did not fare as well as my underwear. I tried it on but the hem now terminated somewhere south of my brassiere and well north of my navel. Gravity and Age, the unsung horsewomen of the apocalypse, had put the skids to my ability to carry off belly shirts years ago. I regretfully folded, petted, and put the now child-sized garment aside. Roger's sweater had shrunk as well, but since it had been too large on me to begin with, I could still easily get away with it.

When I finally managed to hop, wriggle, and squirm my way into everything, I risked a glance in the mirror. I couldn't argue with Kane's assessment. I *did* look like hell. The small, bruised laceration over my eye had started to scab, but the swelling wasn't too bad. I was paler than usual with the exception of my cheeks and lips which still bore the rosy remnants of windburn. Without my extensive collection of brushes and my trusty flat iron, my thick, dark hair tumbled over my shoulders in a riot of loose untamed curls. I found a brush in the vanity drawer and dragged it painfully through the matted mess. Yes, I know women would pay a fortune to get natural curl like mine. It's been pointed out to me at least two million, fourteen thousand, nine hundred and thirty-seven times. Trust me, frazzled poodle is not a look to aspire to, ladies. Finally, though I wasn't exactly poised to grace the cover of a magazine, at least I was dressed, warm, and dry.

I draped the damp towel on the chrome bar, and hung Morgan Kane's flannel shirt on a hook on the wall. I heard the distant slam of a door, followed by heavy footsteps. The smell of coffee tickled my nostrils and made my mouth water. The herbal tea had definitely not done it for me, and while lack of coffee wouldn't kill me, it could be very unhealthy for everyone else.

My ankle stopped squawking once supported by the wrap, allowing me to move independently. Using a toe touch combined with an ungainly limp, and a furniture grab-and-go method, I could maneuver fairly well, and with a much more precise degree of balance. Even so, my awkward hobbling was anything but quiet. Kane had to have heard me coming by the time I stumbled through the kitchen doorway.

The kitchen was lovely with a high beamed ceiling, wide planked pine floors, and a u-shaped granite countertop. The stainless steel appliances were sleek, modern, and obviously top of the line. At the far side of the room a huge fire blazed cheerily in a second fireplace. Morgan Kane sat, frowning, at the head of a large farmhouse table directly in front of the fire. None of the eight chairs around the weathered table belonged to a matched set, yet each was uniquely beautiful in its own way. He leaned forward and pushed a large, steaming mug in my direction. I fell heavily into a chair at his left and pulled the beverage toward me. He nodded at a sugar bowl and a pottery creamer shaped like a cow. You know, one of those touristy souvenir types where the milk comes out of the cow's mouth? Classy.

"Black is fine, thanks." I took a large sip and closed my eyes in ecstatic appreciation. He rescues, he launders, he makes a mean cup of coffee. Was there anything the man couldn't do? Oh yeah, he could send people into the hereafter but couldn't go in and bring them back if he screwed up. That, apparently, was my problem. Yippee.

Kane remained silent as he leaned back in his chair, arms crossed over his chest—his broad, magnificent chest—and gazed out of the window. His jaw looked carved in stone, and a tic I hadn't noticed earlier twitched in his cheek. From this angle, with the damaged side of his face turned away, his unmarred features were striking. *Probably not pertinent to the current situation, right?*

"So, what now?" I mumbled through another big gulp of java. From what Alicia told me, it seemed time was of the essence. I had no idea how much my little Arctic excursion cost me when it came to that commodity. I suspected we should be doing something a bit more urgent than sitting around the fire drinking coffee. Really, really good coffee. It would be a shame to waste the rest of the pot. I wondered if he had a travel mug.

"Now, I explain the finer points of the assignment. Then I show you how to use your necklace to open a portal, cross over, and if all goes well, get back out with your target in tow," Morgan Kane replied shortly, finally deigning to fix that startling green stare on me.

My aching spine seemed to straighten of its own accord as I recognized the calculated, feral gaze. My black wolf! I guess most people would find this discovery shocking and completely unbelievable but given recent events I'd been sucker punched into suspending disbelief. It was cool. I was down with it. No problem-o.

"Oh my God, you're a freaking werewolf?" I screeched, bounding from my chair and hobbling several long steps away from him.

I freely admit I'd spent a good deal of time feeling sorry for myself over the last few years. Following my death and victorious return to the land of the living, I'd worked really hard at pulling myself away from the precipice of the bottomless pit of self-pity. All things considered, I actually had a pretty good life. But honestly, trapped with a bum ankle in an isolated cabin in the middle of a freak blizzard with a Grim Reaper who was also a werewolf, while planning to cross the veil to the other side to rescue my ex-husband from a D.I.E.? Seriously, why me?

"Hellhound, actually," he growled, rising to his feet. My back was against a wall, literally. I had nowhere to go. Then again, at least I had a stable surface against which to support my knocking knees. Glass half full, Max.

"Hellhound, huh?" I retorted cynically with far more swagger than I felt. "Well, all righty then, Cerberus. What say I wait here and have another cup of this awesome coffee while *you* slip into your nifty fur coat and slink on over to the other side to hunt down Roger's lost soul?" Discretion may be the better part of valor, but in my case the predilection for acerbity doesn't exactly lend itself to caution. Sometimes even I don't know what I'll say next. It's a gift.

"Cerberus is a distant relative and not one I affectionately seek out at the family reunion." Morgan Kane continued his slow, deliberate stalk toward me. His green eyes gleamed with an otherworldly glow. "You wanted to know about my scars? Well, let's just say Cerberus wasn't too thrilled to see me the last time I paid him a visit."

"Why?" Yeah, I really did ask. I bought into the whole three headed Guardian of the Gates of Hell thing. It was official. I'd finally reached the point where sanity and psychosis co-exist. It only took a few strides of his long legs to bring us toe to toe. Then he splayed a large palm against the wall on either side of my head and leaned toward me, bringing us almost nose to nose. I could feel the heat radiating from his body. Of course, his whole being a product of Hell might actually give his hotness an entirely new meaning.

"Why? Because he has something that belongs to me and I want it back." For a minute, I thought he would elaborate, but he seemed to think better of it. "Let's go." He pushed back from the wall and jerked his head in the direction of yet another doorway indicating I should follow. "It's time to do this, if you're still planning to get it done."

I hesitated long enough to gulp down the remainder of my coffee, before limping after him. As soon as I crossed the threshold I knew there was something different about this room. My initial impression was that of a cluttered office, but I soon realized I didn't recognize most of the objects scattered on the desk and surrounding tabletops. However, the shiny scythe I glimpsed propped in one corner was pretty self-explanatory. Dark heavy drapes hung at the windows, completely obscuring the world outside, and even the furniture was dark and heavy. The whole room reminded me of something out of a bad horror film. Oddly, there was a row of small, potted dogwood trees blooming along one wall, and I wondered how they managed to survive in the sunless gloom, not to mention the dead of winter. Then again, I was about to cross into the afterlife with a fugly necklace as my vehicle, and the Grim Reaper as my tour guide. A tree blooming out of season in a dark room didn't seem quite so extraordinary, all things considered.

The Grim Reaper—aka Morgan Kane— Hellhound—waited in the far corner in front of a large, oval mirror set into a heavy standing frame. The air reeked of burnt sage and dust. My mother's necklace grew exponentially warmer against my skin the farther I advanced into the room.

"Dang, that's hot. And not in a good way." I impatiently yanked it free to lie outside of Roger's sweater when it became uncomfortable.

"Actually, it *is* in a good way. It means it works. I

had my doubts after learning it had lain dormant all these years." Morgan dragged his fingers through his hair with a relieved smile. Even with the distracting scars, his smile was enough to jumpstart the libido of any normal woman. Fortunately, as we've already determined, I am not a normal woman. I, of course, was immune. That's my story and I'm sticking to it.

"What works?" I frowned up at him as I reached his side and wiped my sweaty palms down the sides of my jeans.

"The amulet. It's a portal passkey. Whenever you're in the vicinity of a portal, it heats up. The closer you are, the hotter it gets. When you touch it to the surface, the portal opens." He patted the glass of the mirror. "The necklace will open this portal to take you into the Between, and when you're ready, it will open another to bring you back. Simple, but effective."

"Simple? Well, I guess when you grow up swimming in the River Styx some fugly necklace allowing you to step through an innocuous mirror into the afterlife isn't terribly impressive. Call me crazy, but I have slightly less confidence in its purported efficacy. What happens if I can't find the mirror again once I'm there?"

"Not a problem," he grunted as he shooed me out of the way and dragged the mirror from its place in the corner and out into the middle of the room. "There are portals all over the Between. Most of the time they're found on or near a reflective surface—windows, mirrors, water. You'll know you're close to one when the amulet starts to heat up. Because you entered through this portal though, no matter which one you use to return from the other side, you'll end up back here."

He positioned the mirror in the middle of the room and motioned me closer. I simply stood there fingering my mother's necklace. I figured I was perfectly fine right where I was. I saw no reason to get any closer to that thing than absolutely necessary and risk being sucked into some otherworldly vortex before I was good and ready. At the risk of sounding redundant, these mystical bozos really had a lot to learn about employee orientation. I hadn't even received a nominal job description. Hadn't they ever heard of job shadowing? Seriously. A little one on one with some poor sap who'd actually *done* this before would not go amiss.

I didn't realize I was mumbling all of this aloud under my breath until Morgan Kane quirked a brow in my direction and chuffed a laugh. At least I think it was a laugh. It started out as a deep rumble in the region of his solar plexis, and ended as a forceful exhalation of air falling somewhere between a snort and a bark.

"Job shadowing?" He shook his head. "That's a new one."

"Apparently it is around here," I snapped. "Did it ever occur to you guys it might be a little disorienting to the average Joe to discover that not only do supernatural beings exist, but that you actually *are* one?"

His eyes widened. "No, frankly I guess it didn't."

"Yeah, well in your position I guess it wouldn't. Newsflash, Rover, it is!"

"Rover?" His brows lowered ominously, and his lips peeled back in a snarl as he started toward me. Shoot, did I say that out loud too? I always say what I mean. The problem is I don't always mean to say it to the world. Maybe I should have warned him there was a distinct possibility my mind to mouth filter was broken today. Apparently finding out I was a supernatural superhero has that effect on me. Who knew? Lack of sleep, unwanted revelations, excessive caffeine, and a body temperature hovering near Eskimo Pie when combined with my escalating anxiety was bound to result in a temporary case of diarrhea-of-the-mouth. This is a serious medical condition, people. It can usually be attributed to a pre-existing diagnosis of shit-for-brains. However, we've already established the circumference of my thighs validates my brilliance, so in my case I'm sure it was probably a fluke.

"Hey." I stepped back slowly and held out my hands palms upward in the universal sign for please don't kill me. "I'm sorry, all right? I didn't mean that the way it sounded. Try to see it from my perspective. There I was, comfortably bundled in my fifteen-hundred count Egyptian cotton bed linens, sleeping peacefully, minding my own business, maybe enjoying an erotic dream or two, and foolishly thinking maybe my life was finally going in the right direction. Suddenly, I'm prodded and poked from a sound sleep by Megawatt-Millie, informed that for all intents and purposes my ex-husband is dead, and now it's time for me to step up to the plate and follow in my supernatural-superhero mother's footsteps and venture into the afterlife. I agree to step up to said plate, drive off in a snow squall that quickly turns into a raging blizzard, miss a deer, hit a tree, nearly freeze to death, pee my pants, and find myself the naked houseguest of the Grim Reaper who also happens to be a Hellhound. Then I am forced to *drink tea*. Now, I'm supposed to step through a *mirror* into the complete unknown without the faintest notion of what to do or how to do it, completely dependent on a fugly necklace to get me home. Is it any wonder I'm a little *testy,* Mr. Kane? It's not even breakfast time, and I've already had it up to *here!*" I held my hand six inches over my head. And yes, I said that all in one breath. "In my defense, I'm short, it doesn't take long."

Morgan Kane stood so close by this time that the hand I jerked over my head nearly smacked him under the chin. I lowered my hand slowly and busied myself by unnecessarily tugging the hem of my sweater down over my jeans. Since the hem already reached my mid-thigh area, it was kind of an empty gesture.

His frown cleared, and his brows rose in the other direction, nearly disappearing into his hairline. His green eyes were wide, his mouth slack, and it opened and closed oddly, like a confused fish out of water. He tugged distractedly on his good ear before closing his eyes and pinching the bridge of his nose between his thumb and forefinger. He may have counted to ten.

"Well, sure it sounds bad when you say it like that," he observed.

The corner of his mouth twitched, and I burst out laughing. I realize it was a completely inappropriate reaction to the situation in which I found myself, but I've never been much of a stickler for convention. I laughed until my stomach cramped, and I had to bend over and grab my knees. I laughed until the tears came to my eyes and poured down my cheeks. I laughed until I began to hyperventilate and gasp for air. I laughed until the Grim Reaper gripped my shoulders, gave me a rough shake, and yelled, "Snap out of it!"

"Damn! That hurt!" I rubbed my smarting shoulder. "You couldn't have just asked me nicely to knock it off?"

"I did. Three times. Look, Ms. Logan, if you don't want to do this just say so. Nobody's holding a gun to your head."

"Of course I don't *want* to do this, *Mr.* Kane," I sighed, swiping at my dripping eyes. "But the unfortunate truth is that what I *want* to do usually has very little bearing on what I actually *have* to do. So can we get on with it before I have enough time to think about it and decide I simply *can't* do it?"

His stare lasted several long heartbeats until he finally nodded.

"Fine. As I said, this mirror will be your portal. You'll go into the Between from this point and when you come back, this is where you'll end up no matter what portal you use to get out. The pilot was scheduled to have a massive myocardial infarction shortly after landing the plane, so don't waste time searching for him. He's probably moved on by now since he died pretty much on schedule. You only need to worry about finding your husband and retrieving one other passenger before the Seekers realize you're there."

"Ex-husband," I clarified. Of course I loved Roger, but Morgan Kane was one hot ticket and I figured I should keep my options open. My bad. I held up a finger. "Hold on. Who are these Seekers?"

"They report to Cerberus. When a soul ends up in the Between, the Seekers go to work trying to corrupt, er, shall we say questionable souls, into choosing the darkness. If they realize you're a Retriever with the potential to cost them a soul, they'll put every obstacle in your path they can. Best to avoid them altogether."

"Gee, ya think?" Truthfully, I was beginning to feel as though my life had become a chapter in a bad comic book adventure series. Sure, I'd always wanted to be one of those tough broad heroines talking shit, packing heat, and kicking ass. I suspected I might have a better chance of pulling it off in leather boots and a bustier than sneakers and Irish knitwear, but a girl's gotta work with what she's given.

"Let's see." I heaved a deep breath. "Get in, find Roger, get out. Avoid Seekers. Got it. Um, how will I know which ones are the Seekers?"

"Diaphanous black shadows that look like big creepy worms."

"Charming. Can't wait to meet them. Let me recap, if I may. Get in, find Roger, get out. Avoid Seekers. Find shiny portal. Use fugly necklace. Get the hell out."

"Roger and Dirk," the Hellhound clarified. "You need to find Roger and get Dirk out."

"*Dirk*? You mean as in *Dirk Kramer*?" Doctor Dirk Kramer fancied himself a ladies' man. Of course, that was his opinion and the notion was highly dependent on one's definition of a lady. At one time he'd been a colleague of Roger's. He'd been hitting on me, and anything with breasts, for the better part of ten years. At least for the ten years I knew him. It hadn't mattered that I was married. Of course, why would it? He was married, too. He was, in a word, scum. Perhaps you've already sensed he is not one of my favorite people?

"Is there a problem?"

Hell, yeah, there was a problem. The last time I'd run into Dirk, I put him in his place firmly and publically. So much so, in fact, he felt compelled to move his practice out of state to escape the certain humiliation and ridicule that was bound to follow. And then of course there was that pesky sexual harassment suit the nurses had worked up the courage to file after they witnessed me taking him down a peg or three. Now I'd been handed the golden opportunity to rid the world, and all decent, self-respecting women, of Dirk Kramer's unwelcome and inappropriate attention for all time, but if I wanted Roger, I also had to locate and save Dirk's slimy ass. Seriously? It struck me as just plain wrong on so many levels.

"Nope, no problem at all," I lied, crossing my fingers behind my back. What? It counts! If these Seekers were hoping to corrupt souls, I figured Dirk was more than halfway there without their influence. "What happens if the Seekers get to him, I mean them, first?"

Morgan Kane's massive shoulders lifted in a shrug. "You can't get a soul back once it's committed to the dark. At that point, the best you can do is damage control and get the hell out."

"Sweet!"

"Are you plotting something, Logan? Because you're going to have your hands full the way it is. Just get in, find them, and get out. No games." Kane's brows knit together in a fierce scowl.

"Get in, find them, and get out. Gotcha!" I mimicked obediently.

"Do you have your fingers crossed behind your back?" His eyes narrowed suspiciously, and he took a step or two in my direction leaning in close to see behind me.

"Pul-eeze! That would be a little childish, don't

you think?" I deliberately widened my eyes and fluttered my lashes in an expression of wounded innocence. What? I didn't say they *weren't* crossed. Whereas he didn't appear convinced, but at least he let the matter drop.

While I'd been busy donning and admiring my lovely lingerie earlier, Morgan Kane had apparently taken the opportunity to replace his weathered flannel shirt with a black tee that clung lovingly to every taut, bulging muscle. He dug his hand into the pocket of his tight jeans, tugging them down just low enough on his slim hips to allow a glimpse of his rock hard abs and one side of that delicious cord of muscle tracing along his hip and disappearing into his waistband. My mouth went dry. I wondered if the Seekers were women? Maybe Morgan Kane could go with me and distract them with his jaw dropping physique while I saved the world? What? It could work. He was sure as hell distracting me.

With a supreme effort worthy of an Academy Award, or something equally shiny and prestigious, I refocused my attention from Morgan's tempting package to the golden object in his palm. It appeared to be a small pocket watch, and when he flipped it open with his thumb, my suspicions were confirmed.

"Take this," he grabbed my wrist and placed the object in my hand, curling my fingers around it. "It's set to alarm ten minutes before your time expires. If you haven't secured the target by then, find a portal and get yourself out."

"Or I turn into a pumpkin?"

"Or the Seekers start calling in back-up."

"Back-up?" I could almost feel my blood pressure

dropping in response to the sudden techno rhythm of my heart. My mouth dried up once again, and this time it had nothing to do with the Grim Reaper's hot crossed buns. I didn't like the sound of that at all. I mean, if I didn't get a trusty side-kick, it didn't seem fair anyone else should. Then again, if I'd learned anything in the past year it was that Fate didn't play fair.

"Cerberus." He offered helpfully. "He really isn't a big fan of Retrievers."

I probably should have been more surprised, but by now my you've-got-to-be-shitting-me meter had given up the ghost. Cerberus. Three-headed Hellhound Guardian of the Gates of Hell. Sure, why not? I scrubbed a hand over my face and swallowed hard. *Well, wasn't that wucking fonderful?*

Chapter Five

I thought I'd reached my saturation point when it came to the unexpected, but I have to admit the result I achieved when I touched my mother's necklace to the mirror was astonishing. The cool, silver sheen slowly changed and morphed into something new. My own image, and the replication of the room behind me, shimmered and faded, before mutating into a thick, swirling vortex of opaque gray fog. I strained and squinted to see what lay beyond the mist, but to no avail. My teeth chattered, though the temperature in the room hadn't changed. This was it. I was an authority when it came to telling everyone else to pull up their big girl panties and get on with it. I really hate when that practice-what-I-preach crap comes back to bite me.

"You sure about this?" Kane asked quietly from somewhere over my left shoulder.

"Of course I'm not sure, you idiot, but I'm going to do it anyway. Any last minute advice?"

"Keep your eye on the time. Get in, find them, and get out."

"Is there an echo in here or do you have such a limited vocabulary that you're compelled to repeat yourself?"

"No offense, Logan, but don't let the portal hit you in the ass," he responded dryly. "And don't forget to close it behind you. I'm planning to take a nap when you leave and prefer not to have it interrupted by unexpected visitors."

"Oh, by all means! I wouldn't dream of disturbing your beauty sleep while I'm busy who-knows-where doing who-knows-what while working against the clock and avoiding worms and three-headed Hellhounds." I could have sworn I heard him stifle a chuckle. I personally didn't see the humor in any of this. A heavy hand dropped briefly on my shoulder and lightly squeezed.

"You can do this, Logan. The gift wouldn't have come to you otherwise. Just remember things aren't always what they seem. Now all you have to do is believe in yourself."

Ha! Easy for him to say. Maybe that was the problem. Oh sure, I'd managed to bargain my way back from the dead. Truthfully, I attributed that marvelous feat more to luck than talent. And I have to admit I really learned something from my little stint as the temporary SSI, and managed to salvage the important relationships in my life before I succeeded in flushing them completely down the crapper. But, c'mon! This was hardly the same thing at all. Well, except for Buddy's suspected involvement, the unfortunate and erroneously dead, and the fact it was up to me to fix someone else's screw up.

I swallowed the pesky bubble of panic wiggling its fingers up into my windpipe. I could do this, of course I could. At least I hoped I could. Okay Maxine, chin up, boobs out, walk proud! I glanced down, and though my back was stiffly arched in an almost perfect imitation of Robin Hood's bow, I saw no appreciable change in the size of my chest. Well, at least my chin was up. I dropped the necklace back inside my sweater, where it rested unpleasantly in my cleavage. I swiped my sweaty palms down the sides of my jeans, one more time, took a deep breath, swallowed hard, and stepped through the haze before I had a chance to change my mind. I faintly heard Morgan calling out, but the sound of his voice, like everything else, was quickly swallowed in the thick fog. I wasn't sure whether I'd imagined it or not. Suddenly I was there—wherever *there* was—in a world existing somewhere between science and superstition.

This new reality stank of silence and age. I turned around and stabbed my necklace into the mist hoping I'd managed to close the portal, but seriously, how was I supposed to know? I turned back and slowly put one foot in front of the other, and tentatively inched forward. When in doubt, act like you know. That's my motto.

An unseen wind swirled the murky vapor into a shifting curtain around me. I forced myself to keep moving as tendrils unwound from the soupy mist and crawled over my skin like living things. Frankly, after the day I'd had, I wasn't sure they *weren't* living things. Goose bumps stood at attention all up and down my arms under the soothing warmth of Roger's heavy sweater. Sounds reached my ears, a faint but obvious din that reminded me of a carnival or street market. I breathed a sigh of relief as the dense vapor slowly dissipated, and at last I saw the Between. I'm not sure what I expected, exactly, but I hadn't counted on something resembling every movie version I'd ever seen of Main Street, U.S.A..

Something seemed slightly off, though I couldn't put my finger on it as smoke and shadow coalesced into figures dressed in every manner and style. There were people everywhere, from every era, walking, standing, sitting in little groups at al fresco tables around a central square. It seemed like a perfectly ordinary scene. And then it hit me. Gray. Absolutely everything was some shade of gray. From purest white to deepest black and every variation in between, there was not a single drop of color to be seen. It was like stepping into the production of a pre-Technicolor movie. Without the caterer. Which was unfortunate.

Hey, even supernatural superheroes need to eat.

Since I had no idea where to start searching for Roger and Dirk, I figured my best bet was to simply ask someone. I began to have second thoughts as I drew closer and realized everyone had ceased their banter and activity and stopped to stare. At least I assumed they were staring since their heads swiveled in my direction as I approached. Of course, none of them seemed to have eyes so I couldn't really be sure if the empty sockets were actually sizing me up. Short people rarely see eye-to-eye with others to begin with, but this was ridiculous. Need I elaborate on how incredibly uncomfortable this was? *Can you spell Twilight Zone, boys and girls?*

I've discovered when I find myself in deep shit, the wisest course of action is to keep my eyes straight ahead, my legs on standby, and my mouth shut. Okay, so I don't always do so well with the keeping my mouth shut part, but there's a first time for everything. As I made my way along the street through the eyeless throng, grasping hands reached out and plucked at my clothes. I pulled my arms in as close to my body as I could, crossed them over my chest, and kept walking. I probably should have asked Morgan Kane a few more questions before embarking on Max's Excellent Adventure. Like maybe what to expect or where to start looking. I know I talk a good game, but some days if my stupidity could be converted into a usable energy source, I could power a small country. Seriously.

"It's your mortal energy that attracts them," observed a scratchy, disembodied voice to my right. "They are enticed by what they've lost and can never have again. They crave life."

I peered through the grayness and saw an old woman on the porch of a tiny, little cottage set back from the street. She swayed to and fro in a creaky, wooden rocking chair. Two long knitting needles clacked away in her gnarled and twisted fingers. Her twinkling eyes observed me from a face as wrinkled and desiccated as a dried apple topped by a mop of wispy, white candy floss hair. Did I mention she had eyes? Hallelujah! I immediately diverted my straight and narrow course, and hurried toward the grandmotherly figure who had spoken.

I approached the cottage and promptly fell up the stairs. Parked cars hit me, floors attack me, poles magically appear in front of me. Yes, I've always been talented like that. Falling downstairs? That's for losers. Falling upstairs? Now that takes major skill!

Granny-Apple-Head never even blinked. She simply continued her rapid and relentless yarn manipulation, and from my new vantage point with my chin on her porch deck, I could see whatever she was working on fell in folds from her lap, continued across the porch, and disappeared somewhere over the rail on the far side. Either she only knew one stitch or she was engineering a scarf for someone with a neck the size of the Equator. I decided I probably didn't want to know.

I climbed painfully to my feet and brushed myself off, waiting for gate control to kick in. The gate control theory of pain was first hypothesized in the early nineteen-sixties. According to this theory, the experience of pain depends on a complex interplay between the central and peripheral nervous systems. Physiologically, pain messages originate in the injured area and flow along the peripheral nerves to the spinal cord and on up to the brain. According to the gate control theory, the pain messages encounter nerve gates in the spinal cord before they can reach the brain for processing. Whether these nerve gates open or close is dependent upon a number of factors, including competing stimuli from other peripheral nerves. The competing stimuli can cause the nerve gate to close, preventing the pain message from getting through to the brain, thus reducing or even completely negating the actual pain experience. To put it in layman's terms, did you ever notice that when you bump your head, rubbing the area seems to provide relief? Gate Control Theory. Case in point, the deep, unrelenting throb in my left knee where it struck the edge of the step, though extremely unpleasant, had the unexpected benefit of completely obliterating my brain's awareness of my sprained ankle. Score!

To my relief, the sightless mob backed off, presumably to resume their previous occupations, whatever those might be. Granny-Apple-Head twitched her endless pile of worsted wool aside, revealing a second chair, and I hobbled over and lowered myself into it gratefully, if not exactly gracefully. A snuffling sound came from the region of my feet. I looked down. A small, tangled bundle of grimy white fur crept out from beneath the chair, sniffed me thoroughly, hopped into my lap, and curled up with a contented sigh.

"Not now, Alia," Granny reprimanded. "Down! There's a good girl." The puppy-like creature jumped off and slinked back under my chair. "She smells the Hellhound on you," the old woman continued matter-of-factly, as though that should explain everything. Uh, huh. Whatever. I was here to rescue Roger, not to serve as a volunteer member of the afterlife ASPCA.

"Speaking of the Hellhound," she continued conversationally. "You see that tree over there? A gift from Kane. You probably noticed some at the house." She waved toward a small dogwood tree growing to the right of the steps. "Cultivates them himself. Odd pastime for a Hellhound if you ask me, which you didn't. The sad part is the blooming season here is so darned short. The flowers don't last nearly as long here as they do on the other side. Did you know that the dogwood flower is a symbol of healing and sacrifice according to legend? It might seem fragile, but it isn't. The stem? That's tough and resilient, resistant to damage. It bends but it doesn't break. All in all dogwood is the total package. Guess maybe it reminded him of me." She laughed uproariously at her own observation.

"I don't want to appear rude, but I didn't come here for a horticulture lesson," I said brusquely.

She sighed. It sounded like someone letting the air out of a balloon. "It was an analogy, Retriever. You obviously are missing the point."

"Apparently. Who are you?" I asked bluntly. I

didn't have time for riddles and analogies. I was on a tight schedule.

"What am I, will you become. What you are, I once was," she cackled happily. Did I mention her voice had the lilting quality of dead leaves being stuffed into a lawn and trash bag?

"So you're what? The Yoda of the afterlife?" I snapped.

"Actually, Maxine, I'm The Timekeeper. And unless I'm very much mistaken, time is something you have in limited quantity at the moment." She leaned toward me with a conspiratorial whisper. "But before you begin your journey, come inside. You must be parched."

Some long forgotten story, some faint but stubborn memory teased the edge of my subconscious. My eyes narrowed suspiciously. I mean, the woman looked like dehydrated fruit. I doubted *she'd* had anything substantial to drink in years. Because I had no idea who I could trust in this extraordinarily odd place, I figured it was better to trust no one at all.

"Wait a minute," I said suddenly as recollection reared up and slapped me in the head. "This isn't one of those places where I eat or drink something and then find out I'm trapped here forever, is it?"

"Don't be ridiculous, dear. You have us confused with Faerie. In the Between, with the exception of a few supernatural beings like yourself, souls check in, but they don't check out, no matter what they consume while they're here. We have no need for cheap tricks."

"Well, um, okay then. I guess I am a little thirsty." What? You try skirting death from hypothermia, tangling with a sexy Hellhound Grim Reaper, and crossing the astral plain to be obscenely groped by the cast of the Zombie Apocalypse and tell me your mouth wouldn't be a little dry. I rest my case. "What've you got?"

"Lemonade and gin." Granny-Apple-Head aka The Timekeeper hauled her not inconsiderable bulk from the rocking chair and set her needles on the seat where they kept right on knitting and purling. I must have looked as astonished as I felt because she seemed compelled to explain. "Time marches on, Maxine."

"I, uh, think I'll take the gin," I stuttered.

She made a tut-tutting noise and shook her head. "Well, dear, it's up to you, but you'll want to have a clear head if Cerberus gets wind of you being here."

"C-C-Cerberus?" I stuttered inanely. "But this is the Between. Cerberus guards the gates of the Underworld, er Hell." Sure Morgan had mentioned him, but I figured as long as I completed my mission in a timely fashion, Cerberus would stay on his little acre and I'd stay in whatever place was farthest away from his little acre.

"Indeed he does," Granny agreed. "But he also has a teensy little problem with the living crossing into any realm of the dead. Kind of a pet peeve, you might say. It really frosts his sulfur spewing butt when one of you gets back out and takes a potential denizen along with you."

Well, isn't that special? I thought of Morgan's scars. If Cerberus could inflict that kind of damage on a Hellhound, what might he do to me? Note to self— remember to thank Morgan Kane for the warning next time I saw him. Assuming there was a next time. Somabitch.

"Make it lemonade," I sighed.

"Wise choice."

The Timekeeper lumbered into the cottage, and the screen door banged closed behind her. My chattering teeth mimicked the rhythm of the clattering needles as they continued to knit the fabric of time. As soon as the Timekeeper disappeared, Blondie slithered out from under the chair to snuffle curiously around my feet once again. When I didn't stop her, she sprang back into my lap and curled against me in a tight, little ball. I was startled to see she had the same clear, green eyes Morgan did. A Hellhound puppy? I guess most people would find it astounding. Me? Um, yeah, at this point, not so much.

As soon as baby Hellhound heard the measured tread heralding The Timekeeper's return, she jumped on my chest, put a dainty paw on each of my shoulders, and gifted me with a heartfelt slurp right up the side of my face. Then she quickly dropped to the floor and crawled back under my chair. I was still scrubbing the slobber from my cheek with the sleeve of Roger's sweater when Granny handed me a tall, frosty glass and gifted the puppy with a frown, letting us both know she wasn't fooled for a minute by Blondie's docile recumbence beneath my butt.

"Cookie?" Granny held out a delicate china plate painted with roses I was certain would be much more attractive in color. The monochromatic treats didn't look especially appetizing, but I figured my chances of finding a Long John in the Between were slim to none. Long John's were my personal favorite, and I just knew the taste of raspberry jam wrapped in a freshly fried doughnut topped with thick white frosting and coconut would somehow make this whole day seem brighter. I must have gotten lost in my fantasy for a minute because The Timekeeper rattled the plate under my nose impatiently. Hmm, black cookie or white cookie? Decisions, decisions. I opted for the black, hoping against hope it was chocolate. It was. In the absence of raspberry jam wrapped in a freshly fried doughnut topped with thick white frosting and coconut, chocolate really was the next best thing.

The wizened woman tossed a cookie to the dog, settled back into her chair, and took up her needles. I scarfed down the cookie and chugged the lemonade. I hated to give the impression I was an ill-mannered glutton, but hey, I had a deadline to consider. I pulled Morgan's watch out of my pocket and glanced at it, stunned to see it had been barely five minutes since I'd left him. It felt like hours. My confusion must have shown in my expression because Granny-Apple-Head chuckled, crooked a finger at herself and said "Timekeeper, remember?"

"Uh, yeah, sure," I replied. I reflected it might be a worthy idea to stay on this girl's good side. "Listen, Timekeeper, I appreciate the hospitality and all, really, but I came here for a reason and I should probably get to it. I don't suppose you have any helpful hints for finding my ex and his vulgar friend, staying off of Cerberus' radar, and getting out of here in one piece all within the specified time constraints?"

"Actually, I might." She smiled and shook her head in amusement. "You remind me so much of your mother on her first retrieval, Maxine. She didn't have a damn clue either. Of course, she was much younger than you are now."

"You knew my mother?" I breathed in disbelief. And really, did she have to bring my age into it. I'm a little touchy on the subject. But, I digress. "Is she…is she here?" I didn't dare to hope. Rightly so, as it happened.

"I'm sorry, dear, but she moved on long ago, as she was meant to," Granny clucked in regret. I tried not to be crushed. After all, the idea of meeting my long dead mother in the afterlife had never even entered my mind until The Timekeeper mentioned her. Still, I felt a fleeting pang for one brief moment that it was not to be.

"Wait a minute, if everyone has to move on, who are all of those…people—and I use that term loosely—who followed me here?"

"The Lost," she tutted sadly. "Desperate to go back, unable to move on. They cling to denial for so long, eventually they can no longer see their final destination. They simply become blinded and stranded in the Between."

Since I knew a thing or two about denial with a capital D, I could empathize with the poor creatures. Fortunately, I'd been able to artfully arbitrate my return from the dead. Apparently, not everyone was so well versed in the stages of grief.

"So where's Roger?"

"Roger and his unsavory friend are at The Crossroads. Sort of the Office of Central Processing on a much grander scale," she chortled. I personally wasn't seeing the humor in any of this. Maybe she was silently telling herself a joke she hadn't heard before?

"So how do I get there, and how do I find them once I do?"

"Just follow the road there. Takes you right to it.

You can't miss it," she assured me.

"It isn't made of yellow bricks by any chance, is it?" I retorted with a smirk.

"Ha, ha. You're a funny girl, Maxine," she answered without any hint of a smile. Apparently she only laughed at her own jokes. "No, of course it isn't made of yellow bricks, but you'd be wise not to stray from it. When you get there, try to find a place your friends would have been most attracted to in life. The dead tend to cling to the familiar."

Blondie crept out from under the chair when I stood and moved down the steps. She stood at the top, watching me, tail wagging, tongue lolling crookedly in one of those comical doggie smiles. I realized she really wasn't a puppy at all, just a rather small, young dog...er, Hellhound?

When I reached the street, her ears pricked up, and she began barking as she paced in agitation from Granny-Apple-Head to the steps and back again.

"She'll be back, Alia," Granny-Apple-Head soothed in a matter-of-fact voice. I fervently hoped someone with clout heard her pronouncement and took it to heart. Her serene sing-song voice did little to calm the anxious animal. Didn't do a whole lot for me either. "Fine!" The old woman threw her hands up in surrender as her needles continued to work the wool. "Go with her if you insist, but I refuse to take responsibility. Kane will not be happy. You know what will happen once you're away from here. Better you stay here where he can't find you, girlie, but you always were a headstrong female."

The animal leapt into The Timekeeper's ample lap and gifted her with the same sloppy affection she'd bestowed on me, before tearing down the stairs and planting her furry little butt happily at my feet.

"Alia, you do know what to do if Cerberus shows up?" Granny-Apple-Head called after us. Alia yipped loudly.

"What *do* we do if Cerberus shows up?" I wasn't fluent in Hellhound so I figured I'd better get the English translation just to be sure we were all on the same page.

"Run like hell, of course," Granny replied pleasantly. *Wucking fonderful.*

I peered down at my unexpected traveling companion. Alia, huh? Yeah, I decided I'd just stick with Blondie. It suited her. Her sharp green eyes gazed back with an eager adoration I doubted I would live up to. Once upon a time I was insecure, now I just try to be realistic about my limitations. She was cute, but at this point I felt like she was simply one more thing for me to worry about. I treated myself to a heavy sigh. It didn't help much.

"C'mon, Blondie. I guess it's you and me against the Underworld."

Chapter Six

I didn't realize how shortsighted I'd been in taking for granted the sadly unrecognized and largely unacknowledged blessings in my mundane and incredibly ordinary day to day existence…until, one day, it wasn't ordinary anymore. A year ago I could never have imagined any turn of events that would find me racing down a foggy road in the afterlife working against a deadline to save the man I loved—accompanied by a raggedy canine who'd appointed herself my new best friend. I have no idea what she saw in me other than the fact I apparently carried Morgan Kane's scent. Maybe that designated me a member of the pack. The Crossroads. Seriously? Undoubtedly some sarcastic bastard's idea of a euphemism.

Though no vertically challenged people with high pitched voices and oddly constructed clothes popped out of the foliage to cheerfully sing us on our way or offer us lollipops, Blondie happily trotted along beside me, ears at attention and tail wagging furiously. She wasn't much of a conversationalist, but at least she was company. I estimated we'd been hoofing along at a brisk clip for at least half an hour, and my ankle was beginning to ache. We hadn't seen a single soul. Yeah, pun intended. There was no scenery to speak of—just the road ahead and what appeared to be bare emptiness falling away on either side. The complete and utter silence unnerved me most, and kept the hair on the back of my neck in a constant state of erect agitation.

I spotted a small pile of boulders rising out of the mist, ahead on the left, and decided it might be my only opportunity to take a rest. Hey, it wasn't like I had a map with rest stops and tourist destinations all penciled in. I veered to the side of the road. My canine companion stayed glued to my side and collapsed on my feet with a sigh even more heartfelt than mine when I finally planted my butt on the unforgiving stone. I regarded the tangled bundle of fur.

"You really aren't very intimidating for a Hellhound," I observed dryly. Blondie picked up her head, wagged her tail, and let out a loud yip I interpreted as agreement. My stomach rumbled. I found myself wishing I'd copped a few of Granny-Apple-Head's cookies for the road. I was never especially good at planning ahead. I was more of a knee jerk reaction kind of girl. I should probably learn to be more proactive. Just saying.

"Okay, Killer, time to get back on the road." I hauled my weary butt up from the rock and almost tripped over Blondie who hesitated a moment longer than was probably wise considering my Bachelor's Degree in Klutzy. I should probably come with a warning label. She managed to get safely out from under my feet with an impressive series of contortions, and we both made it back to the roadway unscathed. I had no idea how much farther The Crossroads might be, so I struggled to keep a steady pace despite my screaming ankle and aching knee. Once we got there, it was anyone's guess how long it might take to locate Roger and Dirk.

Statistically there are over six thousand deaths every day in the United States alone, and I was pretty sure the good old U.S. of A. didn't have a monopoly on the afterlife. Worldwide, the number is closer to one hundred and fifty-five thousand. My best hope was that people were processed in the afterlife according to *people Max is looking for*, and *people Max has no interest in whatsoever.* I didn't think it was likely but then again, it wasn't completely impossible. Remember that glass half full thing? Yeah, well, I mentally slapped a lid on that puppy to conserve every drop and kept putting one foot in front of the other. Sometimes putting one foot in front of the other is the only thing you can do, even if you have no idea where you're going.

I'd already worked up enough of a sweat to be uncomfortably moist when the rain started. One might hypothesize a cool, gentle rain in the middle of a long, sweaty walk might be refreshing.

One would be wrong. Roger's lovely sweater, knitted in a traditional Aran design originating among the nineteenth century fisher-folk of Ireland's west coast, in addition to being stylish, was also renowned for its durability, water resistance, and insulating properties. Notice I said water resistant and not waterproof? And don't forget those nifty insulating properties. Oh, and I should probably mention it was not a gentle rain, it was a blinding deluge. Within minutes I was hot and wet, and not in a good way. The added scent of Eau de Damp Mutt clogging my nostrils courtesy of my traveling companion made the whole experience almost more pleasurable than I could reasonably endure. How could one small dog produce such an overabundance of pure, unadulterated stink?

I glanced down, shocked to discover Blondie's head, which had previously been bobbing somewhere in the region of my knee, was now nearly level with my hip. She'd pretty much doubled in size since we left Granny-Apple-Head's. Damn, I hoped it wasn't a side effect of the cookie. I took a quick inventory. All of my parts seemed unaffected. Oh well, as long as my ass didn't start bulking up, it really didn't matter to me how big my Hellhound got. Heck, if she got big enough, maybe I could saddle her up and pretend she was a pony. At least it would give my throbbing ankle a break.

The rain lasted only long enough to make me miserable. Naturally. The downpour had been intense, and puddles glimmered everywhere. My fugly necklace, which I'd all but forgotten, decided to remind me of its presence by stabbing me unpleasantly in my cleavage. I remembered what Morgan had said about portals—mirrors, windows, water. There must be a portal close by because I felt an increased warmth against my chest that had nothing to do with the mad insulating properties of Irish wool. I thought it might be a good idea to see if I could actually find and open a portal on my own in case we had to make a quick getaway. I slowed my pace and walked to first one puddle and then another, waiting to see if the temperature of the necklace changed.

At last I felt the heat increase, and I carefully approached the suspected portal. I squatted down to peer into the puddle. As my bones creaked and my lower back went into spasm, it occurred to me the real challenge here might be my ability to get back up. But, I digress. When I got a gander at my reflection, I realized I was probably safe in the Between. I was by far the scariest looking thing here. Blondie, who ostensibly never met a puddle she didn't like, padded over to me and plopped down, tongue dripping. I touched my finger cautiously to the water, watching expectantly as the little circles ebbed outward from where I'd disturbed the surface.

Seemed like a normal, unpretentious run of the mill puddle to me. I took a deep breath and held the pendant out over the puddle. Blondie cocked her head to the side, one ear up and the other flapping sideways with that cute *what in the hell is going on* look that dogs have. Yeah, that one. The moment I touched the necklace to the surface of the water it began to shimmer as the mirror had done, but this time, instead of a murky fog, I was staring straight into Morgan Kane's dim gothic room. He paced nervously, throwing a worried glance in the direction of the mirror from time to time like he was waiting for something. Or someone. Me?

As soon as Morgan came into view, Blondie let out a startled yelp and made a dive for the portal. Morgan's head swiveled in the direction of the mirror with a start. I quickly dipped the pendant in the water and closed the portal. Well, he *had* said he didn't want any unexpected guests. Blondie seemed harmless enough to me, but that didn't mean the Hellhound Grim Reaper wanted her to drop by unannounced. She landed in the puddle with an enormous splash that, quite frankly, couldn't possibly make me any wetter. However, I could have lived quite happily without the snootful of mud. As soon as she realized the portal was closed, my canine companion pawed frantically at what was left of the wet patch, whining and sending water flying in every direction until the puddle was completely empty.

"Bad dog," I admonished. "You made the puddle all gone!"

Blondie continued to whine pitifully and kept sniffing at the wet spot where the portal had been, while I ineffectually scrubbed the mud from my eyes. When I looked around, I noticed every one of the puddles was all gone. Well, at any rate I knew the necklace would work. Hopefully there would be a slightly more reliable portal than a quickly evaporating puddle by the time I found Roger.

I checked Morgan's watch. I had just under three hours left. I really wished I had Map-quested The Crossroads and gotten mileage and a time estimate for my little excursion. I pulled my smartphone out of my back pocket and checked the display. No reception. Yeah, I was shocked, too. The Between gave new meaning to the term dead zone.

The road ended abruptly. Well, at least my perception was that it ended abruptly. Honestly, I'm pretty sure I'd been peering at the middle of the road for so long that I probably suffered from highway hypnosis—that altered state of awareness marked by a trance-like state resulting from gazing at a fixed point Don't tell me you've never driven home from work, pulled in the driveway, and had no recollection of how you'd gotten there? It's a relatively commonplace experience when the conscious and unconscious minds are concentrating on different things. A person can travel great distances, respond to external stimuli in the expected manner, and have absolutely no recollection of having done so because the consciousness dissociates. Don't believe me? Just ask my sister,

Denise the Psychology junkie. She'd be quite happy to explain the phenomenon is an example of automaticity according to the study of Cognitive Psychology. One stream of consciousness navigates while the other is preoccupied. Preoccupied? *Moi*? Yeah, you might say I had one or two things on my mind.

My Hellhound and I stood at the edge of a field of tall grass the width of a football field. Of course, tall was a relative term when you're a person who only appears statuesque while standing in a crowd of fourth graders. I could just see over the top if I stood on my tippy-tippy toes. Eureka! Beyond the amber waves of grain lay civilization, or at least what I assumed passed for civilization in the afterlife. Frankly, from my vantage point, it reminded me of Ghost Town in the Glen, the Old West themed amusement park my dad and Stepmother Gail used to take Denise and me to when we were kids. Well, except I couldn't detect a single gunslinger, stagecoach, or rollercoaster. Just my luck there wouldn't be foot longs or caramel corn, either. If I ever had a momentary lapse of sanity and agreed to do this again, I was *so* bringing a box lunch.

The grass extended to both my right and to the left as far as I could see. There didn't appear to be any way around it. My only option was to plow right through the middle. That didn't concern me too much until I noticed the movement. Actually, eerie undulation might be a more accurate description. Not necessarily a bad thing. Or at least it wouldn't be if there was the slightest hint of a breeze. Or if Blondie's ears hadn't flattened against her skull. Or if there wasn't a low, suspicious growl rumbling from her throat. Or if I ignored the fact the weirdly waving wheat resulted from the diaphanous black shadows that look like big creepy worms swirling through the stalks. The road had led me directly to The Crossroads, exactly as Granny-Apple-Head had promised. Our journey thus far had been relatively uneventful. I had a feeling our luck had just changed. And not for the better. Things that seem too good to be true usually are.

A frisson of forewarning punched me low in the gut. My wet, pruney toes instinctively curled into my soggy socks and saturated sneakers. Being clearheaded wasn't all it was cracked up to be. I should have had the gin.

It's a good bet I would have stood on the edge of that field pondering my next move carefully for whatever length of time it required to logically and reasonably consider the wisest course of action. However, I've never actually been accused of being particularly wise. Any attempt at sane and deliberate contemplation flew right out the window when I spotted an all too familiar slick faced teen with a slippery façade of moderate acne and garish purple braces staring at me with a frightened expression from the middle of the field. It was Buddy, the former SuperSave cashier and current rogue G.R.I.T. who had become the bane of my existence.

Buddy, that dirty dog who, in an attempt to impress the bigwigs, caused not only my untimely and erroneous death, but Roger's too, and apparently a goodly number of others. I had no sympathy for his google-eyed look of terror comically magnified by his coke bottle glasses. I felt my lips involuntarily curl back from my teeth in a snarl. Be afraid, Buddy. Be very, very afraid. You think you can do what you want and get away with it, but every dog has its day. Bow Wow Buddy. Maxie's here!

I didn't stop to consider the consequences of plunging into the current domain of the diaphanous black shadows that looked like big creepy worms. I only knew I wanted to feel Buddy's Adam's Apple bobbing beneath my gleefully tightening fingers while I choked the stupid out of him. Chest heaving, arms pumping, sneakers squishing, I plowed into the field and headed straight for the wide-eyed weasel.

The Seekers flocked to me like underage teenagers to a beer keg. Blondie stayed glued to my hip, snapping ineffectually at the swirling creatures. They quickly surrounded me. I could feel their curiosity as they inched closer. When one of them finally touched me, a cold dread invaded my bone marrow. Then suddenly, they darted away and made a beeline for Buddy when he began to run toward the opposite side of the field, away from me and toward The Crossroads. I tripped to a breathless halt as the Seekers surrounded him like a funnel cloud. His head swiveled in my direction, eyes wild. He mouthed the words *help me* before they consumed him completely, and both Buddy and the Seekers disappeared.

Poor Buddy didn't look too happy in the loving embrace of his new friends from the dark side. Guess he should have thought of that a little earlier. Not. My. Problem. So why did I feel an unsettling little twinge of sympathy and concern for the incompetent adolescent that threatened to distract me? Maybe because on some level I realized he was a mixed-up, insecure kid and insecurity is notorious for inspiring poor decisions. Not that I could relate. Nope, not at all.

In any event, I could hardly spare the time or energy to worry about Buddy and his problems at the moment. I had enough of my own. Self-preservation is a peculiarly strong motivator. Now that Buddy had taken his toys and gone home, my path was clear, and it didn't take me long to cross the field and start up the small incline leading to The Crossroads.

The atmosphere was completely different here, almost warm and sunny. Albeit the pale, watery light wasn't nearly as appealing as the hot, golden glow of a crowded beach in July. Still, it was a welcome change from the creepy gray fog with fingers and sudden, skin-soaking downpours. At the top of the incline, I paused to catch my breath and get my bearings. I stood in the middle of a road curving away to both my right and left. Directly ahead of me, another street twisted and contorted up a steep hill—lined with Victorian style buildings that appeared to be a combination of businesses, shops, and restaurants. I couldn't help thinking the recently dead should have more on their minds than shopping and dining, but hey, who was I to judge?

Just as I feared, there were crowds of people everywhere. Blondie pressed tightly against my thigh, and I buried my fingers in the scruff of her neck to keep her close. I didn't know what help she could possibly provide in the greater scheme of things, but I was grateful for the familiarity of her company in this place where I felt so completely alone and unsure. No one paid any attention to Blondie and me, even though I quickly realized she and I were the only ones wearing a pale, fuzzy watercolor tint which made us stand out like a sore thumb. I didn't know if that was good or bad, or even normal. Oh, yeah, like any of this approached normal. Right?

As we wove our way through the newly departed, I couldn't shake the uneasy feeling that even if the crowd seemed to be ignoring me, unseen observers watched from somewhere behind the dark, unblinking windows of the tall, architecturally appealing structures. Roger and I shared a love of Victorian architecture and under other circumstances these buildings were well preserved marvels I might have stopped to study and admire. Oh sure, Roger took his fair share of heckling from his colleagues who preferred sleek and modern, but one of the things I'd always loved about him was his willingness to fly in the face of convention. *Love* about him. One of the things I *love* about him. I swallowed a flutter of fear that set my heart racing when I anxiously realized I was beginning to think about Roger in the past tense. I would find him. Somehow I would find him, and we would go home, and this nightmare would be over. And I guess I'd make an attempt to save Dirk, too, since that was apparently a non-negotiable part of the deal.

Roger was one of those guys who always believed things would work themselves out as they were intended. I was one of those people who always believed anything that could go wrong would. He hauled me from the pits of gloom, and I served as his reality check. We balanced each other that way. I flipped open Morgan's watch and realized time was running out. The task before me seemed impossible. My eyes filled with tears, and I felt myself sliding down the slippery slope of hopelessness. I'd dropped my half full glass somewhere along the road, and it was becoming increasingly difficult to put a positive spin on my current situation—yet failure was not an option.

I maneuvered my way to the fringes of the crowd and plopped my tired butt on the first empty set of stairs I saw. I needed to think. Blondie collapsed at my feet. Tension and disquiet wound my muscles in tight, painful knots. I stretched my legs out in front of me and rotated my head on my shoulders trying to work the kinks out of my neck. It was then I noticed the sign hanging over my head. The Crossroads Visitor and Information Center. Seriously? Figuring I had nothing to lose, I hauled myself to my feet and pushed open the door.

Despite the elegant grandeur of the building's Queen Anne exterior, the little brass bell over the door hadn't stopped tinkling before a serious sense of déjà vu slapped me in the head. Empty cups and old newspapers littered the floor. Orange plastic chairs were chained together along the far wall. The air reeked of burnt coffee and mildew. A long, wooden counter ran along the rear of the space like something you might see in an old general store. It was the Office of Central Processing all over again. The only things missing were the elevators and Marvin Jenks.

I reconsidered the latter conclusion when a small, wiry, man in an ill-fitting gray flannel suit hurried in through the tattered curtain dividing the front office from what I presumed was a back room. He looked grim and harried, though there didn't appear to be much of a crowd. In fact, at the moment, Blondie and I were the only ones awaiting service. His eyes were narrowed behind his thin wire glasses, and a familiar bald scalp peeked out boldly between the strands of his oh-so-sexy comb-over.

"Marvin?" I squeaked in astonishment. Marvin Jenks, the beleaguered clerk of the Office of Central Processing who'd been dazzled by my brilliance, or more accurately baffled by my Kubler-Ross bullshit, when I found myself unexpectedly deceased, had apparently been transferred. Just my luck he seemed to keep turning up in whatever area of the great beyond I found myself. You may recall I'd recently learned from Alicia that Marvin-the-Rat-Boy took me up on my *Offer He Couldn't Refuse* to fill in for Alicia fully anticipating I would fail. He was also the uncle of Buddy-the-Inept. Need I offer further justification for Marvin Jenks and anyone remotely associated with him to have the distinction of being the top crumb on my crumb list?

"Don't mention that traitor's name to me," the dumpy doppelganger grumbled. "And no dogs allowed. Can't you read, Retriever?" He pointedly poked a finger at a faded sign on the wall over his head. "Take a number and I'll be with you shortly."

"She isn't a dog, she's a Hellhound," I argued. "And she's very well behaved." Blondie immediately made a liar out of me by planting her huge, muddy paws on the counter and introducing herself to the irritated man with a long, wet slurp on the side of his face that left his glasses askew. He was not impressed by her spontaneous offer of affection.

"And no I won't take a number. We're the only ones here, and I'm in a hurry."

"That's what they all say," he sputtered as he straightened his glasses and mopped at the friendly slobber with his sleeve. "The person to whom you refer is my twin brother, I'm sorry to admit. We are estranged as you might have guessed. I am Melvin Jenks, fully licensed and bonded afterlife tour guide and Director of the Crossroads Visitor and Information Center."

"I see," I said slowly. "So that makes you Buddy the Weasel's uncle, too?"

"Buddy?" Melvin paled. "You've seen Buddy? When? Where?"

"Yes, I've seen Buddy. I just saw him a little while ago in the field below The Crossroads. My only regret is I wasn't close enough at the time to grab him by the throat and choke some sense into him. He and his dark, squiggly friends, the Seekers, were cavorting through the grass and communing with nature. You'll pardon me if I'm not especially fond of your wayward nephew. Buddy's the one who got me into this whole sordid mess. First he killed me, and now he's taken out my ex-husband and his colleague. You knew I was a Retriever so obviously you know why I'm here."

"No, I don't know why you're here. Because you are a Retriever, I assume you are here to retrieve. I knew you were a Retriever because you and your mangy little friend manifest color. You may have noticed the rest of the population is a little, er, faded. It's this place. It sucks the life right out of you." He chuckled dryly at his own sad joke. Then he sobered. "He must have been trying to get back here," he mused. "Dammit, I didn't have any more luck with that little shit than my totally incompetent brother."

I concluded his ruminations referenced Buddy. At the risk of being redundant, I will state for the record. Not. My. Problem. Once Melvin pointed out what should have been obvious, I realized Blondie and I had never been completely gray like the others. It was her green eyes that had clued me in to her origins as a Hellhound back at Granny-Apple-Head's in the first place. Hey, I'd been a little preoccupied, so sue me.

"Wait a minute, Mel," I cried excitedly as a sudden thought occurred to me. What? It happens. "So all I have to do to find my targets, Roger McCoy and Dirk Kramer, is keep my eyes open for two guys who still have some color? If I've been sent to retrieve them they should still be connected to the living, and if they're still connected to the living, they should have color, right?"

"Theoretically," Melvin mumbled uncomfortably. "But they won't be the only ones. And the longer they've been here and the closer they are to becoming irretrievable, the less obvious their color will be, so I'm not sure that will be much help. Still, I guess, maybe it does narrow it down. I gather you're new to this?"

"Gee, what was your first clue?" I drawled. Hey, I realize my sarcasm switch has a hair trigger. I would love to be nice all the time, really, but sometimes circumstances just won't allow it. *I'm working on it, okay?* "Any chance you could provide me with a hint on where to start?" Fully cognizant of Morgan's watch ticking away in the pocket of my jeans, I felt it grow exponentially heavier with every minute that passed.

"Well, perhaps I could if you were a little less offensive," Melvin Jenks sniffed haughtily.

Wisely, I remained silent. Yeah, yeah, I know we've established I've never actually been accused of being particularly wise, but I occasionally have my moments and right now I didn't have time to deal with a self-important fully licensed and bonded afterlife tour guide and his ruffled feelings. I already had a full dance card. Sometimes silence is the intelligent person's best way out of a conversation with an idiot.

Melvin magnanimously decided to interpret my suddenly tight lipped lack of response as an apology. He peered at me expectantly for a heartbeat, then reached under the counter and pulled out a large, dusty ledger that looked as though it hadn't seen the light of day in eons. He adjusted his glasses and began a leisurely perusal of the pages, running a finger deliberately down each column before flipping to the next. The process was painfully slow. Blondie planted a restraining paw over my impatiently tapping toes, perhaps correctly assuming my obvious exasperation would only incite Melvin to undertake an even slower pace. If that was possible.

Finally, with a grunt of satisfaction, he slammed the ledger closed, producing a cloud of dust that found its way right into my nostrils, irritating my nasal mucosa, and immediately producing multiple spasmodic involuntary expulsions of air from my mouth and nose accompanied by a fine spray of spittle that projected several feet. I couldn't stop sneezing. It happened so suddenly I didn't even have a chance to politely cover my mouth. I hoped if I was brewing something contagious, it found a home in Melvin Jenks and his entire supernaturally annoying family. Conflicting superstitions relate the sneeze to evil spirits. There are various belief systems that hold to the notion a sneeze could release the soul, leading to its capture by evil spirits, or that evil spirits could enter the body through the open mouth of a sneezing individual.

Others believed sneezing casts out sins or evil spirits that had taken residence within the body and an immediate blessing is required to prevent the expelled spirits from re-entering the body. You get the picture. The Ancient Greeks, however, believed a sneeze was a favorable and prophetic sign from the gods, an indication of impending victory or success. I decided to put my money on the Greeks. I had a feeling I would need all the help I could get.

"Well?" I prompted as Melvin removed his wire-rimmed specs and ignored me, while he meticulously polished away the wet remnants of my sneezing jag with a handkerchief pulled from the inside pocket of his wrinkled suit jacket. Finally he tucked the handkerchief back in his pocket, readjusted his spectacles, and replaced the ledger beneath the counter.

"Well, I have some good news and some bad news," Melvin began in an oddly regretful voice. "It appears both Roger McCoy and Dirk Kramer have indeed been registered and are still residents of The Crossroads. That's the good news. The bad news is you are running out of time, Retriever. However, it appears the Kramer fellow may be nearby. He was last accounted for in the red light district. McCoy is a bit farther afield, in the processing area for children and adolescents, which is all the way at the top of the hill near the lake. Assuming he's still there. You should concentrate on Kramer first, since he's much closer. Once you've retrieved him, you can go in search of McCoy."

"Why can't I go after Roger first?" I argued. "Roger is far more important to me than Dirk Kramer."

"That would require you to backtrack. It would

cost you more time than you have left, Retriever. If you've run across the Seekers, then they've reported back by now, and Cerberus already knows you're here. Believe me, he's counting the seconds just as you are, and he won't hesitate to come after you the moment your time runs out," Melvin warned. "If that happens, no one will be saved, including you. I don't make the rules."

Blondie whined pitifully and pawed at my leg as if to emphasize how emphatically she agreed with Melvin's assessment of the situation. Damn, damn, and double damn.

"Where is this red light district, and is it what I think it is?" I growled.

"Bottom of the hill, make a right. Can't miss it. And yes, Miss Logan," Melvin smirked as I turned for the door. "It's exactly what you think it is." Of course it was. What else would it be? Granny-Apple-Head had told me the dead cling to the familiar. An afterlife filled with wild and willing women would most certainly be Dirk Kramer's idea of Heaven. I guess some people never learn. Fine. I'd play by the rules for now, but I couldn't help feeling he was not worth the time it would take to save him. Apparently even mostly dead he was still a total pig.

Chapter Seven

Blondie and I beat a hasty retreat and started back down the hill. At least there wasn't any traffic to dodge. Apparently the impracticality of importing fuel to the afterlife precluded mechanical transportation. The only means of conveyance I saw in the dusty streets, besides a pedestrian one, was the occasional horse and buggy. Apparently animals really did move on to the afterlife just as people did. My sister Denise would be ecstatic to learn this. Clinique, her Petit Basset Griffon Vendéen, occupied a spot in her heart only slightly below that of her husband, Brad-the-Famous-Vascular-Surgeon, her twins, Mick and Vick, and on a good day, yours truly. Yes, my sister named her dog after a cosmetic company. I believe I may have already mentioned my sister's penchant for all things retail?

My stomach grumbled loudly as Blondie and I stalked back down the street to the intersection at the bottom. I made myself a promise then and there that the next time I ventured into the great beyond, I was eating a large, decadent meal that left my arteries screaming in protest, and drinking at least a gallon of something cold and wet, and preferably mind numbing, before I crossed over. Of course, it wouldn't be an issue as I was absolutely never doing this again. I didn't care if I was genetically predisposed, morally obligated, or temporarily insane. Once I got back to the physical world, I was cuddling up with Roger under my comfy cotton sheets for an unspecified period of time and doing something unquestionably physical and life affirming.

I would be striking the surname Jenks from all conscious memory and tearing the "J" listings out of my phone book. I was scrupulously avoiding all Hellhounds, hot, blonde, or otherwise. I am a cat person, people. I am never venturing into a quivering mirror, a groping fog, or a dusty, orange-chaired Visitor's Center again. Period. Well, unless it involved someone I cared about. Or maybe some poor innocent child. Or would get Buddy-the-Weasel in a passel of trouble. Okay, so he was in trouble already, but with him who knew what could happen, so maybe I wouldn't rule out a return engagement entirely, but it would be a long, long time from now in the far, far distant future. Even then I wasn't making any promises.

It took forever to reach the end of the street and turn right. We hadn't gone very far before I realized Melvin Jenks had been accurate on one count, at least. I couldn't miss my intended destination, even without the pulsating red globes in every window. No architectural finesse had been wasted in this part of town. The buildings were little more than ramshackle wooden boxes held together with iron nails and the stink of sin. A treacherous plank walkway ran the length of the street, and groups of garishly made up women in long, antiquated gowns spilled with equal impunity from both the doorways and their dresses.

Blondie maintained a constant low rumble under her breath as we wove our way through the watching women. I use that term loosely. It was clear their intense gaze made her just as uncomfortable as it made me. My canine companion even snapped at one who had the poor judgment to get a little too close. *Good doggie.* The woman backed away with an eerie hiss. A sound that made a lot more sense when I noticed all of them had pupils that were little more than vertical slits in their overlarge irises. None of them blinked and if they did I had an uneasy feeling their eyelids would snap up from the bottom instead of drifting down in a flutter of flirtatious lashes as mine were wont to do. Human? I think not. Some kind of supernatural snake people? Probably.

I racked my brain to recall anything I'd ever read about serpents, snakes, and mythology. Lamiae, perhaps? That would certainly explain the floor length gowns and the weird undulations of their upper bodies. The whole scene reminded me of an amateur belly dancing class gone bad. At the risk of being redundant, again I say, I guess it should have surprised me the creatures actually existed. *Unsurprisingly,* Dirk Kramer, asshat extraordinaire, had gravitated to a harem of non-heavenly hoes, with the bodies of serpents and overlarge mythically enhanced mammalian breasts, who seduced men and then fed on their blood. God, I hate snakes. Truthfully, knowing Dirk I'd feared worse. Which should give you some insight into my opinion of Dirk Kramer, Proctologist.

I passed one particularly loud and obnoxious—well, shall we call it a brothel for lack of a more descriptive term? I wrinkled my nose as I detected a familiar scent in the air. Dirk Kramer generally wore enough cologne to induce an asthma attack. Dirk is one of those more is better kind of guys. He disdained the notion of discreetly applying cologne in favor of marinating in it. I was pretty sure he bought it by the case. Or in fifty gallon drums. On the upside, it made him fairly easy to locate in a crowd. You simply had to follow the wheezing.

As I approached the doorway from which the unmistakable stench emanated, a rather buxom blonde doing the serpentine shuffle suddenly blocked the door. Oh, who am I kidding? Compared to me they were all buxom. I took my consolation in the fact they were all destined to develop Cooper's Droop when the weight of their luscious ladies stretched the supporting ligaments of their bosoms to the point of no return. Yep, sooner or later those bodacious baubles were going to be sagging low enough to tickle their navels—while my modest girls would remain perpetually perky. I hope. But, again, I digress.

"Don't look her in the eyes, Blondie," I warned in a stage whisper. "She's trying to mesmerize us. Sorry, Cupcake, your feminine wiles only work on men. We are ladies, and we are immune. Step aside please, I have an asshole to retrieve."

"S-s-s-stop right where you are, Retriever." Her little forked tongue protruded through a set of choppers that hinted at a really great dental plan. Even the fangs sparkled. "You're too late, he's-s-s ours-s-s-s."

"Your lips are moving but all I hear is blah, blah, blah," I bluffed. I nudged Blondie, and she sprang forward, planting her dinner plate sized paws on the Lamina's shoulders and pushing her backwards and out of the doorway.

"Outta my way, bitch," I snarled. "I'm wearing my sassy pants, and I'm working on a deadline."

Her furious hiss gained the attention of everyone in the room. All eyes were on Blondie and me—the angry snake eyes, the shocked Dirk eyes, and the glassy dead eyes of the fellow in the corner with half of his neck already chewed away by the three serpent chicks draped over his body. Apparently his soul had already left the building. The cookie and lemonade I had at Granny-Apple-Head's rushed back up into my throat to say hello. I swallowed them down with an effort and tore my eyes away from the grisly scene. My throat burned like fire. *Focus, Max, focus.*

Dirk recovered from the surprise of my appearance and predictably returned his full attention to the two tremendous sets of tempting hooters nearly engulfing his head. As usual, his ability to think was confined to the limited range of his own little one-eyed snake. I bunched my hands in Roger's sweater and tugged it down in an effort to sop up the profuse perspiration that had been accumulating on my palms since I walked in the door. It was just a hunch, but I figured it was probably a bad idea to show fear. Not a do-able idea, just a bad one. I finally planted my hands on my hips in a threatening stance thinking that might keep the sweat from dripping on the floor and giving me away.

"Well, Dirk," I sniggered in a shaky voice. Try pulling off a snigger in a shaky voice sometime. It takes skill. "I see the Viagra is working out really well for you."

"Don't listen to her, ladies. Big Dirk is all natural, no pharmaceutical assistance required."

"Really?" I couldn't help the amused anticipation lacing my tone. I think maybe it was an allergic reaction to his stupidity. "I would have sworn you were using something."

"Why?" He took the bait precisely as I expected he would. So predictable. For a man who graduated from medical school, he really isn't very bright. He just makes it so easy.

"Because impossible as it seems, you're an even bigger dick now than you were the last time I saw you." Sometimes I just crack myself up. Seriously.

Dirk's brows drew together in an annoyed frown. "Go away, Maxine. You had your chance and you blew it. Can't you see I'm busy?" He gazed hungrily from Thing One to Thing Two. "I must have done something right since I've apparently died and gone to Heaven."

"You know what, Dirk? I get it. You are an Asshole with a capital A. You don't have to keep proving it to me. You *have* died, but this isn't Heaven. If you must know, it's the portal to Hell, and you and your overactive libido are about to let these surgically enhanced reptiles drag you right through the front door." I quirked a brow in disbelief as one of the Lamina glanced down at her bulging breasts and actually opened her pointy toothed mouth to argue. "Oh, pul-eeze, you don't actually expect me to believe those are real, do you?"

Her mouth snapped closed, and she averted her eyes as a deep stain crept into her face. Yeah, thought so. I refocused my attention on Dirk. "You think you're about to get laid? Sorry to disappoint you. If we don't get out of here right now, the only thing you're likely to get is eaten. And not in a good way, Dirk, so don't go getting all excited. Now, unless you'd prefer to stay dead, and end up like your horny little friend over there, let's go. Now."

Thing One and Thing Two reared up in a menacing way. At least that left Dirk in the clear to make a break for it. Assuming he managed to snap the hell out of it, that is. My knees felt like rubber, but I knew if I gave an inch they would take a mile. Or possibly my throat. To my relief, the three munching on the doomed guy had gone back to their meal and weren't paying much attention. Now all I had to do was keep the other two distracted long enough for Dirk to get clear of them.

Dirk glanced over to the corner I had indicated, and his eyes widened in sudden understanding. A horrified expression came over his face. Bingo! Welcome back to reality, Asshat. I jerked my head in the direction of the door. Dirk froze in fear and didn't move. I guess I should have remembered he was never very adept at taking a hint. I so did not have time for this.

"Got any bright ideas?" I whispered to Blondie out of the side of my mouth, gangster-style. She regarded me thoughtfully with one ear up and one ear down, her head cocked to the side, and her great, pink tongue lolling. Damn, she really was cute. Blondie tipped her head back, and a rumble started deep in her chest. By the time it reached her pursed doggie lips, it had turned into a high pitched howl that snapped the serpentine sluts to attention *tout suite*. All five clapped their claws over their ears and slithered back against the wall in a tangled huddle, trying desperately to escape the sound. Guess it wasn't in their key. Good doggie.

"Move it, Dirk," I growled in frustration. "Now!"

Dirk Kramer did a remarkable imitation of a crab as he quickly slid from the chair and scrambled clear of the Scaly Sisters. He jerked to his feet, and high-tailed it for the door. One would think he would be chivalrous enough to at least linger momentarily at the threshold to make sure Blondie and I were able to make our own escape since we'd saved his horny ass. One would be wrong. As we backed out the door, I saw that not only had he failed to linger, Dirk had already hoofed it halfway up the street. He didn't waste any time looking back, and he was picking up speed. I couldn't help noticing he ran like a girl. At least he had sense enough to be headed in the right direction.

The moment Blondie paused for breath the Lamiae struggled valiantly to untangle themselves and made an angry beeline in our direction, fangs bared and forked tongues flickering. I had the uneasy feeling I was about to learn the true meaning of hissy fit. I grabbed my canine companion by the ear, and we took off after Dirk like a shot.

Since I had a natural aversion to exercise, it wasn't long before I ran out of steam. My legs turned to lead. My lungs felt too small to hold the amount of air needed to sustain life. After my brush with death, I'd managed to kick my occasional cigarette habit— mostly. But I still hadn't worked up the nerve, nor the ambition, to join a gym. Now that I was a supernatural superhero, I should probably consider it. Doubled over on shaky legs, gasping for air, really put the skids to the kick-ass image I was aiming for. The ratty tennis shoes and stretched out sweater weren't helping, either. I swore when I got back, I was heading right to the mall for leathers and boots.

Dirk had gotten quite a head start. I knew there was no way I was going to catch him. But neither could I afford to lose him. There wouldn't be enough time to find him again. With four legs to my two, Blondie was far fleeter of foot and, dare I say it? Younger. At least I assumed she was younger. She'd started the day as a puppy, after all. I sent her ahead to round up the douche-bag. By the time I staggered up, Dirk lay flat on the ground, pinned by Blondie's enormous and less than pristine paws, bawling like a baby. What a wuss. Just saying.

"Look, Dirk, I have to find Roger, and I really don't have time for this. How about you knock off the ass-hattery and get up and cooperate like a big boy?" I coaxed in the most patient voice I could muster. Somehow it didn't come out sounding quite as kindly as I intended. Oh well, sue me. Have I mentioned how much I dislike this guy? Some people make you want to knock their teeth so far down their throat that they'll have to drop their pants to chew their food. Dirk would be one of those. Blondie backed off enough to give Dirk the space to climb to his feet. He didn't move. He lay in the dust, blubbering incoherently. I would love to be nice all the time, but sometimes people just won't allow for niceties.

"C'mon, Dirk, up you get," I reached down and tugged on his sleeve none too gently. "I know you think you're a player, but in this game, I'm the coach and we follow my rules. Now get up and get your act together. We have to find Roger and then we all have to get out of here. Personally, I would've been just as happy to leave you right where I found you, but retrieving you was part of the deal, and I'm not about to do anything that will jeopardize Roger." I have a hard time feeling sorry for people when they get what they deserve, but hey, I was trying. Really.

"I don't know why you have to be so snarky all the

time, Maxine," he sniffed, clambering awkwardly to his feet at last. "What did I ever do to you, anyway?"

There are moments when *seriously* punctuated by a question mark is really the only appropriate response. Sometimes the occasion calls for it to be repeated. Multiple times. In an exasperated tone. My encounter with Dirk in the hospital hallway months ago had apparently slipped his mind.

"Is that a rhetorical question? You know what, Dirk? It's not what I say it's how you take it. If the stuff that comes out of my mouth offends you, just think of all the things I keep to myself. As for what you ever did to me? I can't even believe you have to ask. For someone with such a big head, you really should be smarter. Now, unless you'd like to stay dead, let's get moving. I saved you once against my better judgment. Trust me, it won't happen twice. I say jump, you jump, got it?"

I spun on my heel and stomped off in the direction of the Crossroads Visitor and Information Center. Dirk fell into step behind me with Blondie bringing up the rear keeping close tabs on him. I could have sworn she rolled her eyes. She definitely had Dirk's number. Well, she was female, after all. Smart doggie.

I swiveled my head and sneaked a glance at Dirk from the corner of my eye. He shuffled along behind me, head down, dusty, disheveled, and defeated. I felt a funny little niggle in my mid-sternal region that might have been sympathy. After all, he might be a dirt bag but I was relatively sure he hadn't started the day with any anticipation of ending it dead and at the mercy of reptiles with boobs. Then he mumbled something under his breath about wondering what Roger had ever seen in me, and the sensation quickly evaporated. I concluded it was probably just a touch of indigestion caused by the lemonade I consumed at Granny-Apple-Head's. Citrus fruit and I are not friends.

The hill to The Crossroads Visitor and Information Center seemed to have doubled in size since I first went up and back down on my reluctant mission to retrieve Dirk. The crowd had also thinned significantly. I wondered if all of the people I'd seen earlier had moved on to some other celestial plane. The thought caused my stomach to cramp in unease. What if there was a regular schedule or something, and they took Roger to another locale before I found him? Well, if they did, I was going to file a formal complaint. I mean, I'd been sent here with the understanding that I had a specific period of time to work with. Hopefully, some omniscient being had the inside track and knew pissing me off would be far more trouble than it was worth at this point. Nevertheless, I forced myself to walk faster, somehow knowing I could count on my faithful sidekick Blondie to herd Dirk along behind me, but my legs felt like two stiff clubs made of lead no matter how quickly I tried to move.

I finally reached the elegant Queen Anne, and ignoring the closed sign, I put my shoulder to the door and forced it open. The little bell over the door hadn't even stopped tinkling before I realized Karma had screwed with me once again. The empty cups and old newspapers still littered the floor, and the orange chairs were still imprisoned along the far wall. The long, wooden counter still ran along the rear of the room. But, there was a big hand-lettered sign that hadn't been there before. Closed for the Season.

Seriously? I was tired. I was hungry. I was distraught. I was brewing a raging sinus headache from the nose hair wilting onslaught of Dirk's cologne. I wasted no time in hauling my dragging butt over the counter. I dramatically swept aside the tattered curtain and stepped into the back room, clenched fists on my hips, ready to take on Melvin Jenks and anyone else who might be foolish enough to be hanging around or get in my way. My bad-ass entrance was wasted. Apparently the employees of The Crossroads Visitor and Information Center had gotten the memo that a frustrated Retriever with PMS was in the neighborhood.

A lumpy mattress huddled in the corner stripped of linens, the cupboards stood open and bare. Dishes wearing the remnants of a congealing meal were jumbled in the sink. Melvin had apparently left in a bit of a hurry. The faint throb behind my eyes became more pronounced by the minute. The only thing I knew was Roger had last been seen in the processing area for children and adolescents. What I didn't know was where that might be. I stomped my foot in frustration which only caused my head to pound more emphatically. I spun back toward the outer room. Then I saw the map mounted over the doorway.

I stretched up on my toes using every millimeter of verticality I'd been born with, and barely reached the bottom corner of the frame. I batted at it wildly, until, after several failed and rather ungraceful attempts, accompanied by a litany of curses that would have curled Stepmother Gail's hair into a permanent wave, I finally managed to dislodge it from the rusty nail it hung on. I deftly—okay luckily—ducked out of the way just in time as the whole thing hit the floor, and the glass shattered into a million pieces.

"Maxine, are you all right?" Dirk's voice was thick with more concern than I would ever have given him credit for being capable of. Then again I was his nearly dead soul's one way ticket back to his body somewhere in the snowy mountains of Colorado, so maybe he figured he should suck up a little.

"Fine." So not true. "I'll be there in a sec."

I carefully brushed the remaining glass fragments away from the map and pried a corner loose with my thumbnail. The damn thing started to crumble immediately. Obviously I wasn't going to be able to fold it up and tuck it in my pocket. On to Plan B. Squinting painfully to decipher the faded writing, I searched frantically for something that might designate the processing area for children and adolescents. I started at the big red "X" that indicated I was *here* and ran my finger along the street and up the hill since that was the direction Melvin had indicated earlier. It was no easy task since I'd foolishly left my glasses in my bag at the Grim Reaper's place. Who knew I'd have time for recreational reading in the Between?

I carefully lifted the whole frame off the floor being careful not to cut myself on the wickedly pointy shards of glass. I mean, who knows what kind of funky multidrug resistant organisms might be lurking in this place? I so did not need a raging and incurable infection. Well, at least not now. Maybe I would consider it on the second Tuesday of next week when I would hopefully be safe and comfy and permanently ensconced back in my bedroom burrowed deeply under my bed linens. Preferably with Roger.

I pushed aside the tattered curtain and carefully

placed the map on the counter in the front office. I still couldn't see a kick in the ass without my glasses but at least the light coming through the dusty front windows was slightly better than it had been in the back room.

Dirk slumped morosely in one of the orange plastic chairs as uncertain and miserable as I'd ever seen him. Blondie lay sprawled across his feet, presumably to ensure he didn't try to make a break for it. She picked up her head and wagged her tail with such delighted enthusiasm upon my return to the front office that the ensuing cloud of dust she generated threatened to suffocate me. I have to admit, I found her unwarranted affection for me kind of touching. I mean, I've had Sir Chicken Caesar for years, and he barely bothers to crack an eyelid to acknowledge my presence unless there's food involved. I wondered if I could take her home with me.

"What now?" Dirk whispered looking at me with an expectant expression that made my heart thump painfully against my ribs. What now indeed? The one person who could point me in Roger's direction had taken a powder, and I was acutely aware time was running out. Remember when Alicia broke the news I had superpowers and I had the rash thought that with a shiny cape and tiara I could save the world? I was kidding. I couldn't save the world. Heck, most days I wasn't even sure I could save myself. Whose half-assed idea had it been to nominate me to save anyone?

"Now we find Roger and then we go home," I replied with far more confidence than I felt. This pronouncement brought on another tail wagging jag on Blondie's part, which in turn triggered a sneezing fit from Dirk. I kept my eyes glued to the map as my finger traced a dusty path looking for a place-name that might indicate a processing area for children and adolescents. Wait! Hadn't Melvin mentioned a lake? Surely a lake would be indicated on a map.

I covertly blinked back the tears welling up in my eyes and obscuring my vision. I was blindly walking a road I would never have expected to travel. Hell, who was I kidding? It was a road I wouldn't have ever have imagined existed. Yet I couldn't afford to give into the encroaching despair. I couldn't let myself accept I might stumble, that I might not make it through. I found Dirk and I *would* find Roger. I could figure this out. I was directionally challenged, not brain dead. Sometimes strength isn't a raging bonfire, it's just a tiny little flame that whispers *you got this.* I listened for a whisper, but heard nothing except deafening silence.

"I'm getting kind of hungry," Dirk whined suddenly. "Isn't there anyplace to grab something to eat around here?"

"Really, Dirk? Do you maybe have to pee, too? Could you stop thinking about yourself for five minutes and think about the bigger picture?"

"But I just realized I haven't eaten since…well, maybe yesterday." Dirk's handsome features twisted into an unattractive expression of concentration as he tried to reconstruct the details of the last twenty-four hours. "Put yourself in my position, Maxine. I just found out I'm possibly dead. I almost got eaten by well-endowed snake women. It's been a trying day. Some protein would not be unwelcome."

"I'm trying to see things from your point of view, Dirk, but there's only room in your ass for one head at a time, and yours is already there." Sometimes it's nice to not think before speaking. That way I'm just as surprised as everyone else at what comes out of my mouth.

"Apparently you are still dwelling on the unpleasant exchange we had in the hospital hallway some months back. I'm obviously the bigger person here since I've been able to let it go, despite the major disruptions it caused in my life. You really need to move on, Maxine. Holding a grudge is not a healthy thing. I'm sure it hurts you far more than it hurts me." Dirk didn't meet my eyes while he gave his little speech.

"Really, Dirk? You think that one little encounter is the reason you make my skin crawl? Sorry, that actually has very little to do with it. I don't know," I pondered thoughtfully as I slowly and deliberately approached him where he sat slumped in the chair studiously examining the dust on his designer loafers. "Maybe it's the way you wear your hair. Or maybe it's the color of your eyes. More than likely, it's the fact you've been hitting on anything that wiggles, giggles, or jiggles for as long as I've known you. No, Dirk, I'm not holding a grudge. I'm keeping a list and remembering everything so when it's my turn to drive the karma bus I know exactly who to run over!"

He did look at me then.

"You know something, Maxine? You have no business driving the karma bus. You think you have things all figured out, but you have no insight at all into what people are really like. Hell, you thought Roger was cheating! If there is any person on earth less likely to do something that isn't above board, it's Roger. I know it, your family knows it…hell, every doctor and nurse and cafeteria worker in the hospital knows it. Yet you were married to him for thirteen freaking years and didn't have enough common sense to realize it."

"I realized it eventually," I retorted stiffly. "I was dealing with a lot at the time, Dirk. I may have been feeling a little…well, anyway I might have been wrong. I understand that now. Anyway, common sense is overrated and usually has very little to do with emotionally influenced perceptions."

"That's my point, exactly," Dirk announced in a nauseatingly superior tone. "Everyone is dealing with something, Max. Everyone has issues. Unless you have the inside track on what those issues are, maybe you shouldn't be so quick to judge."

I looked to Blondie for support. She appeared to be thoroughly engrossed in a spot on the ceiling. I wasn't sure if she'd stopped paying attention or if she was subtly avoiding my gaze because she agreed with Dirk.

"Okay, Dirk." I crossed my arms over my chest and quirked a brow. "Enlighten me. What issue entitles you to be a serial cheater?" I knew time continued ticking away, but I couldn't help myself. I had to see what justification Dirk would offer for his overall sleaziness.

"I'm not," he replied quietly.

"Huh?"

"I'm not a serial cheater. In fact, I'm not a cheater at all. I've never been unfaithful to Nancy. Not once."

"Oh, please, Dirk. You don't honestly expect me to believe that! Did you forget who you're talking to? I've seen you in action. Hell, I've been on the receiving end of the action." Of all the excuses I expected, complete denial wasn't even in the mix.

"Believe me or don't, Maxine. It doesn't really matter," Dirk replied in a weary voice and climbed stiffly to his feet. "My point is, you judge people on assumptions based on what you perceive to be the truth—not facts based on any actual knowledge. Maybe I've simply been trying to prove to myself that I've still got it. Now, have you figured out what our next move is? I think I'd really like to get out of here."

Dirk glanced uneasily in the direction of the curtain separating the office from the back room. Something creaked and rustled. Blondie rose from her sentry duty at his feet and planted her paws on the counter, a low growl emanating from the back of her throat as she stared at the doorway. The curtain rippled, and a dark shadow crept underneath. Seekers.

I stared hard at Dirk. Maybe it was the jade in my mother's fugly necklace at work. Alicia had said it would help me sense the truth in all situations. Maybe it was just that I'd never seen him so tired and vulnerable. But, somehow, I knew he was telling the truth. At any rate, his fidelity and his issues had no bearing on our current situation. We needed to move, and we needed to do it now. I glanced at the map and desperately prayed the tiny blue blob due north of our present location was the lake I sought and not simply the sloppy remains of Melvin Jenks' lunch. I stepped forward and grabbed Dirk's clammy hand, whistling Blondie to my side as a second dark shape worked its way beneath the fabric.

"C'mon, troops," I ordered in a shaky voice, dragging them both in the direction of the door. "We have a Proctologist to retrieve."

Chapter Eight

My blood sang with urgency as Dirk and I elbowed our way up the hill through the milling crowd. I saw no further sign of the diaphanous black shadows that look like big creepy worms, but I knew they were out there—somewhere, watching and waiting. Blondie seemed to know it, too. Her ears remained flattened against her skull, and she led the charge, nosing a path through the purposeless throng, and glancing back over her shoulder every few minutes to make sure me and Dirk kept up.

Dirk retreated into silence and simply followed my lead, putting one foot in front of the other without question or comment. I found his company a lot less offensive when he kept his mouth shut. Maybe I was almost ready to acknowledge he wasn't quite as abhorrent as I'd originally surmised, but I still thought his methods for improving his self-esteem were sleazy and selfish and left a lot to be desired.

By the time we reached the top of the hill, I had no choice but to stop for a minute and catch my breath. Bending forward at the waist, I clutched my midsection and noisily sucked air in through my clenched teeth. My legs burned, and my chest ached. I wasn't sure whether it was due to the exertion, or the barely suppressed fear of failure.

"You know, Maxine, you really should think about

joining a gym." Dirk eyed my backside. The fact he wasn't even winded did not endear him to me, not at all.

"I am not fat, Kramer. I'm simply so sexy it overflows." I straightened up with a groan and glanced around. Both the buildings and the crowds had thinned out. The road ahead was surrounded on both sides by trees that creaked and rustled ominously even though I couldn't detect any breeze.

"I was remarking on your obviously pitiful endurance, Maxine, not the size of your ass," Dirk replied, punctuating his explanation with an eye roll for good measure

"Oh, yeah? Well, just so you know skinny girls freeze to death faster."

"Duly noted." Dirk Kramer grinned at me. I detected no hint of speculation or ulterior motive in his expression. Without his usual sexually inappropriate overtones, he appeared almost friendly, and dare I think it—charming? It was entirely possible Dirk Kramer and I were having a moment. I found the idea even more implausible and only slightly less palatable, than the notion I'd been born with supernatural superpowers. But there it was.

Have I mentioned I don't do change?

Blondie trotted back to Dirk and me, and nudged my hip in the direction of the road. She fixed me with a worried green stare and whined softly. Yeah, yeah, I get it. Time to get moving. Subtle doggie. She ran on ahead as Dirk and I resumed the trek.

After a few minutes of brisk walking bordering on a jog, I saw the end of the tree line and made out a glint of water ahead. The lake! My forgotten jewel warmed my boobs. I staggered forward in relief. I'd done it! Now to find Roger and get the hell out of here.

I reached for Dirk's hand. Hey, after the day I've had, can you really begrudge me a moment of temporary insanity? I dragged him behind me to where Blondie had paused to wait. We were about to step out of the trees and head toward the playground I'd already spied near the water's edge, when Blondie froze. The hair on her neck jumped to attention. She crouched low to the ground and backed up slowly until she'd maneuvered her body between Dirk and me and whoever, or whatever, crashed through the underbrush in our direction. The low, threatening growl emanating from my baby Hellhound only confirmed my worst fear that whatever was approaching was not the Crossroads welcoming committee.

I knew exactly who it was the minute he stepped from the trees and into the middle of the road. Even though he sported only one head at the moment, his neck was definitely thick enough to support three. The wide leather dog collar with the wicked silver spikes was a dead giveaway. In human form at the moment, he was a man women would find compelling with dark hair, dark eyes, and attractively rough-hewn features. Not to mention the massive and muscular physique. Honestly, it should be illegal for bad to look so good. But it was hard to discount the evil swirling around him like a cold, dark cloud.

On second glance, I realized it was actually the Seekers streaming out from between the trees and gathering around their leader. Anyway, as far as I was concerned, it completed obliterated any semblance of charm or appeal. Larger even than Morgan Kane, his massive body was encased entirely in black leather, his chest so broad he could barely cross his arms over its width.

Dirk's fingers tightened convulsively on mine, and I became aware of a rhythmic tapping. It took me a minute to realize it was the sound of my teeth chattering. Cerberus apparently heard it too, and his lips peeled back from his teeth in a smile cold enough to freeze lava.

"So you're the new Retriever," The Gatekeeper's voice boomed painfully against my eardrums and echoed through the surrounding forest. "Pardon me while I color myself unimpressed."

"Pardon me while I don't give a shit," I retorted. Okay, who said that? I innocently swiveled my head from left to right waiting for the careless fool to own up. Seriously. It just tumbled out of my mouth with no premeditation whatsoever. I had no idea what possessed me. Frankly, I was as shocked as anyone to discover I still retained the ability to speak.

Dirk swallowed audibly at my side, and Blondie buried her face in her paws. A deep, threatening snarl rumbled up from Cerberus' colossal chest. First he howled, and then he began to bark. I squeezed my eyes closed and braced myself for a protracted and painful death.

Seconds later, when I found myself still breathing, I dared to crack a lid. To my utter astonishment, the Hellhound had been nearly incapacitated by a fit of laughter. Finally, he gave an ugly snort and assumed his formerly threatening expression.

"Well, Retriever, aren't you are an amusing surprise? Still little people who ride high horses usually end up getting hurt on the long way down. You shouldn't stir up crap when you don't have the toilet paper to clean it up, sweetheart. That one was scheduled to be mine." He nodded his dark head in Dirk's direction. What little color Dirk still sported left his face in an instant, and his hand grew icy cold in mine. I swallowed hard, realizing the eminent proctologist was going to be absolutely no help whatsoever. He was literally scared stiff. I tugged on his hand to pull him closer and slightly behind me.

"*Was* is the operative word here, Gatekeeper. Even an asshat like Dirk deserves a second chance."

Considering my own epic fails, Dirk was probably right. I had no business judging anyone. It was a lesson I thought I'd learned after my last foray into the great beyond, but apparently not in Dirk's case. I also remembered he and Nancy had lost a child to cancer a little over ten years ago. Coincidence? Maybe, maybe not. Maybe that which doesn't kill us doesn't always make us stronger, maybe sometimes it just turns us into asshats. I sure as hell wasn't ready to make Dirk Kramer my new best friend, but I wasn't about to hand him over to the Gatekeeper of Hell, either.

"Besides," I continued with renewed confidence. "I may be new to this whole retrieval thing, but I do know you can't touch us until I run out of time, right? And I still have—" Morgan Kane's pocket watch chimed jarringly.

"Ten minutes," Cerberus finished with a smirk. "You're correct, Retriever. I can't touch either you or your target until time runs out." His hand shot out so quickly I barely even saw it coming. I ducked instinctively but it wasn't me he reached for. He grabbed Blondie by the scruff of her neck and held her helplessly dangling in the air between us. "But I can touch *her*."

He shook Blondie roughly. She hung there like a limp, defeated rag-doll.

"You should have stayed hidden behind the old woman's skirts, Alia. Now you're mine. Kane was a fool to think an inexperienced Retriever had any chance of helping you escape me and get back to the other side."

"Hey!" I took a step toward him. "That's *my* dog. You put her down right now!"

"With pleasure." He sneered and slammed her to the ground where she landed with a pained yelp, before going completely still. I stepped toward her, but Cerberus reached down and tossed her behind him like she weighed no more than a feather. My heart sank as the Seekers swirled around her.

"Tick tock, Retriever. See you in…" He paused and checked his wrist. "Nine minutes." And then they were gone. All of them. Including Blondie. I choked back a sob. How could I leave her? Maybe I wasn't as much of a cat person as I previously thought. Sir Chicken Caesar would be crushed. I stood there, helplessly staring at the spot where she'd been only seconds ago.

"Nine minutes, Max," Dirk said in a strangled voice. "Nine minutes and then that…thing is coming back for us. We have to get out of here. Now." He took off jogging in the direction of the lake.

I dragged the back of my hand across my eyes. Dirk was right. His palpable panic somehow counteracted my own. Kane had said the power wouldn't have come to me if I couldn't do this. Therefore, the Grim Reaper believed I could. I had to believe I could, too. I would find Roger. I would send him and Dirk back to their lives. And then I would find Cerberus and get my damn dog back.

Maybe the rules said I only had nine minutes to complete my task and then I was fair game for Cerberus. Well, I was pretty sure no one had mentioned there were any rules that allowed a big pile of smoking brimstone to help himself to my canine companion, either. And if there were? Then the rules were stupid. I hated the rules. I decided I was making my own rules from now on.

Fueled by anger and determination, my legs carried me without cramp or complaint as I quickly gained on Dirk, and then passed him entirely. We burst out of the trees with an energy born of desperation, and my head spun with giddy relief. A large, placid lake lapped gently at the shore where it sloped down. Trees surrounded the water for the most part, but in the clearing there was a playground filled with children who laughed and played, climbing on the jungle gym and squealing on the swings as they pumped their chubby little legs to go higher and higher.

I spotted Roger right away. It was impossible to miss him, seated on a flat rock near the water's edge and framed by a grove of young pine trees. A group of children surrounded him, all appearing to be under the age of ten. They were more subdued than the children on the playground equipment, and clung to Roger like confused little barnacles to a boat. I wondered if perhaps they'd only recently arrived and hadn't quite figured out what was going on.

Leave it to my Roger to be their life preserver in a sea of doubt. It was…well, it was just so Roger. Watching him, concern replaced my initial relief. Unlike Dirk, Blondie, and myself, Roger had assumed the grayscale normal of the Between. I couldn't detect even a hint of color on him and…was he glowing? My heart raced. Maybe it was simply that we were cutting it pretty close to the deadline. Yeah, that must be the reason. He looked up when I called his name and smiled. I took off running in his direction, followed closely by Dirk who seemed a bit put out that I was suddenly winning. As the distance between me and the lake fell away, my fugly necklace heated up until I feared it might brand me. I tugged it outside of my sweater as I ran and it bounced along against my heaving chest to the rhythm of my pumping legs.

If my brother-in-law, Brad-The-Famous-Vascular-Surgeon could see me now, sprinting across a field of grass and clover with nary a cramp or twinge, I felt sure he would be suitably impressed. Brad never missed an opportunity to imply the inevitable leg cramps I suffered every time I climbed the steep flight of stairs to my apartment was due to significant atherosclerotic blockages in the blood vessels of my legs—the only outcome a woman of my advancing age, questionable diet, and the half a pack a day habit I'd recently kicked, could realistically expect. Yeah, those were his exact words. I know, right? Remind me sometime to tell you about the black cashmere socks he wears with sandals. My sister, Denise, is one lucky woman.

The children scattered as I launched myself at Roger without slowing down, and I could finally breathe normally for the first time in forever as his arms closed around me. He buried his face in my hair, which I was quite sure both looked and smelled incredibly delightful by this time, but he didn't seem to mind. I felt his chest expand as he simply breathed me in. The embrace didn't last nearly long enough before he pulled back. Dirk loped up beside us and bent forward, squeezing his knees and struggling for air.

"Who needs a gym now, asshat?" I grinned.

"I see your lips moving but all I hear is blah, blah, blah," Dirk huffed, slowly levering himself into an upright position.

"You made it," Roger announced unnecessarily.

"Of course I made it, oh ye of little faith. Now just give me one minute to open the portal and we can get the hell out of here and go home." I stretched up to kiss his cheek and turned toward the lake. Then I stopped and turned back.

"Wait a minute. You knew I was coming? How could you possibly know I was coming?"

Roger smiled, and I tried not to notice it didn't really reach his eyes. Something wasn't right. He should be surprised to see me, but happy to know we were going home. Shouldn't he?

"I know a lot of things I didn't before. I always thought you were pretty amazing, Max, but I guess I really had no idea. Go ahead and open the portal, honey. Dirk needs to get back."

"We all need to get back," I corrected firmly and dipped my necklace into the waves lapping gently at the shoreline. The water immediately began to churn and foam before settling into a swirling gray fog. When I turned back, Dirk's eyes were enormous.

"What in the hell is that?"

"That's your ticket back to your life, Dirk. Dive on in, the water's fine. Oh, and by the way, it's probably a good idea if you don't mention any of this to anyone when you get back," I cautioned.

"He won't remember most of it, and no one will believe what little of it he does," Roger predicted. "Go ahead and jump in, Dirk. Time is almost up. It'll be fine, I promise. Take care, Buddy."

Dirk cautiously dipped his foot in the water. His eyes widened even more as his gaze skittered back to me.

"Max?"

"Go ahead, Dirk. It's all right, we'll be right behind you," I assured him.

Dirk was always so cocky and brash, it was odd to see him so painfully uncertain. I was surprised to find I actually felt sorry for him. What? It could happen. I knew he'd be fine. He just didn't know it yet. One more step and it would be almost like none of this had ever happened to him. He looked at me again, and I nodded encouragingly. With a final terrified glance at Roger, Dirk took a deep breath, closed his eyes, and jumped. And then he was gone.

I released a deep breath I hadn't even been aware I held and reached for Roger's hand. A strange sense of unease uncurled somewhere low in the pit of my stomach and slowly crept up to wrap a hand around my windpipe. Dirk had been clueless when I showed up. How did Roger happen to know so much?

"It's your turn, Max," Roger said with a sigh.

"Our turn," I corrected, tugging on his hand once again. He didn't budge. He shook his head sadly and pulled me back into his arms. He trembled from head to toe. And then I knew.

"No, *your* turn, honey. I won't be going with you. I was never meant to."

I opened my mouth to deny it, but my throat was busy working through the dry heaves, and nothing came up but air. Sweat broke out on my forehead and trickled from my armpits and between my breasts. I gulped convulsively and pulled back to look at him. His expression sad but resigned. It was the same look I'd seen on his face the day we learned we would never have children. Roger had always been more accepting of inevitability than I could ever be.

"Don't you dare do that," I cried, thumping his chest with my fists as hot tears scalded my face. "Don't you dare look at me with sad puppy eyes, give up, and ask me to accept this, Roger. I can't. In fact, I won't. This isn't the free clinic, this isn't Somalia. You can't help anyone here, Roger. This is dead! Stop acting like this is good-bye, a done deal, over. It's time to come home. You're only thirty-nine years old. We have reservations at Alfredo's on Friday. I just picked up your dry cleaning. You promised to take Caesar to the vet next week. Your patients need you. Your parents need...I need..."

I couldn't get the words out. My lungs felt like they'd shrunk. I couldn't take in enough air. Denial with a capital D had served me well before. I was so parking my ass smack dab in the middle of it now.

"Hey, I had a great ride, Max," Roger said as though I hadn't spoken. "I fell in love with the most incredible woman and against all odds, she fell in love with me, too. What we've had together, Max, is more than some people ever get. Quality always trumps quantity, sweetheart. I think deep down I always knew I wouldn't be growing old. Maybe it's why it always seemed so important to cram everything I could into the time I had. I have no regrets, honey. None. Besides, Nancy is going to need Dirk a whole lot more than you're going to need me."

"I don't care about Dirk. I don't care about Nancy. I really don't care about Dirk," I reiterated firmly in case anyone listening had gotten confused by my temporary softening toward him. "I care about you. I care about us. I love you, Roger. Please don't do this. Please don't ask me to do this."

"You don't mean that, Max. I know you. You aren't a selfish person. You wouldn't be here now if you were. I know you love me, but you don't really need me, not anymore. You'll be fine, I promise. You're strong and you're fierce and you have something you were born to do. I always thought you were special, but a supernatural superhero? Who knew?"

"Well, I don't accept it! I'm taking you back and no one better try to stop me." I glared at the circle of children who simply continued to watch us curiously. I wasn't very big, yet, I felt pretty confident I could take on any one of them if they made a move to stop me. Okay, they were kids and I wouldn't actually hurt them. But I wouldn't allow them to stand in my way either. Desperation and logic have never been friends.

"You don't have a choice, Max." Roger said softly. Who decided I didn't have a choice? I was tired of situations in which I didn't have a choice. Damn it, why didn't I ever get a choice?

"This can't be right, Roger," I insisted desperately.

"It must be a mistake. I was sent here to find *both* of you."

"To *find* both of us maybe, but no one said you were supposed to *retrieve* both of us."

"Of course they did, they said—" But, wait. Had anyone ever actually said I was being sent to retrieve both of them? I scoured my brain. Alicia, Morgan, Granny-Apple Head—they'd all said I needed to find both of them. And...*find* both of them. Oh, God! No! No, no, no!

"You were only ever meant to retrieve one of us, Max. I was never meant to leave here."

"Then why? Why did they send me to find you? Why did they let me think..." Then it hit me. I narrowed my eyes. "They knew I wouldn't come for Dirk if you weren't part of the deal, didn't they?"

"I don't know. Maybe." Roger's beautiful brown eyes crinkled when he smiled. "But, I know you better than that. Your conscience would have won out in the end. No, Max, you were sent to find me because I *asked* that you be sent to find me. A lot is being asked of you. I thought you deserved the chance to say goodbye."

"I deserve a lot of things, Roger. Losing you isn't one of them. The chance to say goodbye won't make that any easier. Nothing can make that any easier."

"I know you think that now, Max. But it will. Maybe not today, maybe not tomorrow, but eventually."

He cupped my face and kissed me deeply, and when the sharp tang of salt burned my tongue I wasn't sure if I tasted his tears or mine. He drew back and smoothed my hair away from my face and gently pressed his lips to each damp cheek.

"Maxine Esmeralda Logan, I have loved you since the moment I saw you across a lecture hall chomping on a pencil, and I always will. But my time is over, and this is where I'm supposed to be. I knew it the moment I arrived. It wasn't where I expected to be, not yet anyway. But I recognize I can't change it. If it was a question of choice I would always choose you. Maybe it sounds trite at the moment, but everything happens for a reason. This isn't me mouthing platitudes. It isn't even me giving up. It's me accepting what is and can't be changed. You need to find a way to do that, too. If you can't do it for yourself, then do it for me. How can I find peace if I know you're out there unable to get past the grief?"

"I can't do this, Roger, I swear I can't." I shook my head so emphatically I imagined I could hear my brain rattling around against my skull. It hurt. Hell, everything hurt, but nothing more than my heart.

"Yes, you can, Max. You're stronger than you've ever given yourself credit for. You're tough and resilient. You bend, but you don't break."

Where had I heard that before? I couldn't think about it now, it wasn't important. What was important was convincing Roger he couldn't stay here. He had to come home with me.

"How do you expect me to forget someone who's given me so much to remember, Roger? How can you ask me to? How do you expect me to go back to a world without you in it?"

"I'm not asking you to forget me, Max. I think it might break my heart if you did. I'm just asking you to let me go. When you're able to think about it clearly, you'll realize it isn't the same thing at all. But it's something you have to do. For both our sakes. It's natural to grieve for what we've lost, but then you have to just be thankful for the time we had and learn to move forward. You need to let me go and live your life, find someone to love, do great things, and above all be happy."

I sobbed openly now because I recognized his resolve. He had accepted what I could not. He wasn't coming with me. No matter what I said, no matter what I did. Roger McCoy had died on that snowy mountaintop where I fervently hoped Dirk Kramer was currently freezing his useless saved-from-death-by-yours-truly ass off. Roger's death hadn't been in error as I was led to believe, and I couldn't retrieve him. So this was it, this was the defining moment when I had to accept the outcome was no longer in my hands. Apparently it never had been. There was nothing I could say, nothing I could do. They'd lied. Alicia, Morgan Kane, Granny-Apple-Head…every last one of them had lied and let me think I could save Roger. My head understood, but my heart hurt. My heart hurt with a pain I wasn't sure I would survive.

"He who has gone, so we but cherish his memory, abides with us, more potent, nay, more present than the living man," Roger whispered into my hair as he pulled me against him.

"Don't you dare quote Saint-Exupery at me, Roger McCoy," I sobbed. "No memory is the same as holding you in my arms. It isn't the same thing at all."

"I know." He smiled through the tears finally coursing down his face. "But in the end, memories are all any of us really have, so we have to make sure that they're enough. And we have great memories, Max, wonderful memories. I'll carry them with me forever. Now it's time to kiss me good-bye, honey. We have company coming, and you have to go."

I suddenly realized the children had scampered back into the trees and dark, squirming shadows were slithering in to take their place. Cerberus.

"Wait a minute, Roger! What if I don't go? What if my time runs out and I simply have to stay here with you?"

"That's not the way it works. If your time runs out, you don't get to stay with me, you get to spend eternity communing with Cerberus. He can't hurt me, but he can sure as hell hurt you. Max, just remember letting go doesn't mean you love someone less. Now kiss me, quick! You have to go." He pulled me close and took my lips. I clung to him with a desperation I didn't know I could feel. I would never have this again. I would never feel him again. He would be gone.

Roger raised his head and cupped my cheek, staring at me intently as though memorizing every detail, as though this final look would have to last forever. And I guessed it would.

He stepped away, and I felt as though someone had kicked me square in the gut with steel toed boots. The pain was so acute and so unbearable I doubled over and wrapped my arms around myself. All the Denial with a capital D hadn't helped a bit this time. I was even having difficulty holding on to my Anger with a capital A. Grief jumped into the mix and pushed every other step in the process aside. It kicked all my good intentions and capital letters to the curb. And Roger was telling me I had to find Acceptance? I couldn't even wrap my head around where that fell in the taxonomy. I didn't want to disappoint him, but I really wasn't sure I would ever find the strength.

"Time's up, Retriever," growled a voice far too close for comfort. "Your ass is mine."

"Go, Max! Go now!" Roger yelled, shoving me away as Cerberus reached for me. Blondie stood behind him, tethered to a leash held by none other than Buddy-the-Weasel. Poor Buddy didn't look so good. In fact, he looked positively miserable. Well, get in line, Dipwad. I couldn't have Roger? Well, Buddy and his sulfur spewing boss were not getting my dog.

"Blondie, come!" I yelled, taking a quick step back toward the water and away from Cerberus. Her ears perked up, and her jaws opened wide. She clamped her gleaming white fangs squarely onto Buddy's scrawny wrist. He dropped the leash with a yowl. My heroic Hellhound launched herself straight at me. I barely had time to glance back at Roger, who mouthed *I love you, be happy*, before Blondie's paws landed on my shoulders and her forward motion, combined with her weight, knocked us both backwards into the lake and out of Cerberus' reach. As my doggie and I tumbled together through the portal, I heard Roger's voice calling out one last time over Cerberus' roar of frustration. He sounded almost amused.

"I thought you were a cat person."

I re-entered the world of the living with a bang, much harder than I might have done if I wasn't assisted by the mass and momentum of a two hundred pound canine. As my head cracked on the floor, I strongly suspected I might have sustained another fatal head wound. Maybe I'd be reunited with Roger sooner rather than later. The thought had merit but it did nothing to lessen the blinding pain shooting through my skull. Blondie bounced off of me and straight into the arms of a startled and relieved Grim Reaper. *So glad I could break your fall, girlfriend!*

After ruffling her fur affectionately, Morgan Kane pushed Blondie down and away and squatted beside me. I opened my mouth, winding up to give him a piece of my mind, but his face wavered, the room spun, and everything went dark.

Chapter Nine

The first thing that hit me when I opened my eyes was a major case of déjà vu. I lay on a sofa, swaddled like a papoose in heavy quilts, in a shadowed room whose only light came from a blazing fireplace. A man squatted in front of the fire, adding wood, his flannel covered back toward me. He was huge. He was hot. He still had a great ass. He was Morgan Kane, the Grim Reaper. He was a big fat liar. I closed my eyes and tried to convince myself it had all been a horrible dream brought on by hypothermia. I tried to believe I hadn't traveled through the portal yet. I clung desperately to the hope Roger still waited for me to bring him home. Then I opened my eyes again and Morgan Kane's sad, green gaze confirmed the truth I was so not ready to face.

He watched me with an odd stillness, as if waiting for me to fall apart, and not entirely sure what to do. He shouldn't have been so worried. He obviously had no idea I was simply not like other girls. I don't do tears and emotion and angst even when my heart has just been torn right out of my chest. Not in public anyway and certainly not in front of the Grim Reaper. Nope, Morgan Kane didn't have to worry about me. I simply didn't do hysteria. My throat ached and my eyes filled. It must be the wood smoke. I looked away.

"How do you feel?" The worn plank floor creaked,

and then he was right next to me—holding a steaming mug under my nose. I struggled to a sitting position, relieved to find myself fully clothed this time, and took it from his hand. At least he hadn't added insult to injury by bringing me tea. There was no denying the man made a mean cup of coffee, but at the moment it was his only redeeming quality as far as I was concerned. Well, that and his phenomenal ass. But, I digress. And right now I couldn't afford to digress. I needed to focus. I needed to stay angry and nurse my sense of betrayal. Morgan Kane's shapely ass? Yeah, right at this moment the only thing I wanted to do was drop kick him on it so hard he'd need a passport to get back.

I took a long, fortifying sip, set the cup on the table, and threw back the quilts. The cold engulfing me couldn't be chased away by a couple of layers of cotton and batting.

"How do you think I feel?" I fixed him with what I hoped was an accusatory stare. My swollen eyes and sopping lashes might have ruined the menacing effect I was going for. Kane's massive shoulders slowly lifted and fell. I climbed slowly and carefully to my feet. I arched my back and rolled my shoulders. I pointedly and deliberately rotated my bad ankle and flexed my bruised knee. I stretched my arms over my head and bent from side to side. "Well, let's see, I'm pretty sore, but I suppose I'll live. Which I guess is more than I can say for Roger, isn't it?"

"I'm sorry, Logan." He reached out and dropped a big hand on my shoulder. I shrugged it off and stepped out of his reach. He simply stood there looking bewildered and acutely uncomfortable. He let his arm fall back to his side and shifted from one foot to the other. Clearly Morgan was more familiar with inflicting death than dealing with the fallout. Well, far be it from me to make it easier on him. My reserve tank of compassion was bone dry.

"You're going to go there? Seriously? Well, to quote your bigger, uglier cousin Cerberus—pardon me while I color myself unimpressed. There's no reason for you to be sorry, Kane. After all, you got what you wanted. You all got what you wanted...you, Alicia, Dirk. You used me, you all used me. You're not sorry, Reaper, not for me. You're just sorry I found out it was never about Roger and me. It was all about what was in it for everyone else."

"That's not true, Logan."

"Isn't it? Well, let's recap, shall we? There I was snoring soundly, minding my own business, perhaps enjoying a vaguely erotic dream or two, when I was poked and prodded with pointy shoes and pretty feet right out of my nice, warm bed by a tiki torch and forced to completely re-evaluate everything I've ever believed about myself and my family. Then I was sent out into a freakin' blizzard with a sadistic electronic navigator, nearly died of exposure, was forced to *drink tea*, then hustled my ass over to another reality without a single clue of where to go or what to do when I got there. Did I hesitate? Did I ask millions of questions? Did I request a little time to think about it?

Hell, no! I stepped up to the plate like a good little team player and did what I had to do. Because Alicia, you, Granny-Apple-Head all gave me just enough information to make me believe I was the only hope for someone I love. When in reality I was the only hope for someone I generally despise. The someone I love was already dead. Oh, and I suppose there were bonus points involved if everything went according to plan and I could save your little blonde Hellhound from Cerberus, too. Every last one of you knew saving Roger was an exercise in futility from the very beginning, but no one thought that was something it might have been nice to share with *me*. Does that about sum it up, Mr. Kane? Did I leave anything out?"

Morgan Kane clenched his jaw and shook his head. "You don't understand, Logan."

"Actually, I think I understand perfectly. You basically set me up and now you expect me to believe you're sorry. Well, you'll have to excuse my skepticism. I might be young, but I wasn't born yesterday."

Turning my back on the Grim Reaper, I limped to the window and tore back the heavy insulated drapery. The storm had ended sometime during the night and left the world dusted in a carpet of powdered sugar. My breath caught in my throat at the beauty of the wild scene. Pristine hills of virgin snow undulated into the distance marred only by the intersecting paths of animal tracks and stands of naked hardwoods dripping with lacy veils of ice. In the distance, the Endless Mountains loomed. A blue-gray backdrop of silver-capped peaks stood sentinel over the forests and valleys below.

The morning sky was a bright, azure blue punctuated by white marshmallow clouds. A trio of blue jays injected a shock of bright color into the landscape, their belligerent bickering punctuating the otherwise peaceful scene. I almost smiled as they argued aggressively over a few sad acorns still dangling from an otherwise unclothed oak just behind the house.

The tranquil beauty mocked me. It should be gray and dismal—the way I felt inside. A gust of wind sent a fine spray of powder skittering across the twinkling surface, twisting whirlpools through the trees and grasping at forgotten leaves clinging to sleeping branches. The leaves I could relate to. I felt the same— dry, helpless, and at the mercy of an indifferent breeze.

"What time is it?" I asked without turning around. The scarred wooden floor creaked again.

"About nine thirty." His voice behind me sounded much closer than I'd expected. "I had your truck towed to a garage. The owner is a friend of mine. He'll take it wherever you want. You can let me know and I'll take care of it."

"It's not mine, it's…" Roger's. I started to say it was Roger's, but Roger was gone. The truck and everything else, aside from an account he'd earmarked for his parents, belonged to me now. He'd gotten all of his affairs in order and given me his Power of Attorney when he'd taken his first trip to Somalia. Every time he'd left I made myself sick with worry, convinced something would happen and he'd never come back. Even under the auspices of a humanitarian organization, the healthcare and relief workers routinely received threats and intimidation from the insurgents.

How many times had I played the scene out in my mind? The phone call that would come, the faceless, sympathetic voice that would break the news, the plain pine box being unloaded from the cargo bay of a charter plane while I stood stiffly at attention on the tarmac, and Roger's mother sobbed into my shoulder. I suddenly realized on some level, part of me had been rehearsing for this for months. And now here I was on opening night, the curtain rising, and I wished to hell I had an understudy because I wasn't sure I could actually go on with the show.

"Logan?" From the tone of his voice, I knew he'd had to repeat himself more than once.

"Yeah, that's fine."

"I asked you if you wanted anything…maybe something to eat?"

I let the curtain fall back into place and turned from the window, temporarily blinded by the sharp contrast between the sunny brilliance of the winter landscape and the darkness of the fire lit room. When my eyes finally adjusted, my view was obscured by a solid wall of plaid. I nearly bumped my nose on Kane's chest. He now stood so close I was pinned against the window. I tilted my head back and stared him straight in the eyes.

"No, Reaper. I don't want something to eat. What I want is to go home and climb into my bed and curl up in a ball. I want to sleep like a ninety-nine year old grandma in a Southern church in August. I want to wake up six months from now and have all of this behind me. Alternately, I want the Timekeeper to unravel about ten feet of her freakin' scarf and let me go back and stop Roger from going to Colorado. I want this to all be a bad dream. I want to be the insecure, slightly irrational, but tentatively happy girl I was yesterday. I want to be the person I always thought I was. I may not have been perfect, but at least I was normal. I want the life I planned. That's what I want, Reaper. You have a couple of cans of *that* in your kitchen?"

Kane sighed and combed his fingers through his

hair but he didn't step back. Nor did he answer right away. Well, I hadn't really been expecting an answer anyway. What could he possibly say? After all he could hardly fire up the stove and whip me up a steaming batch of this-has-all-been-a-really-big-joke. In death Roger had seemed to gain the wisdom of the ages, an understanding and acceptance of things as they were meant to be. I wished he'd had the foresight to share a little bit of it with me.

Everything happens for a reason? Well, those reasons always had and still did hover somewhere beyond my sphere of understanding. In that respect, I guess I was just like everyone else. Even my supernatural superpowers gained me no insight. I knew I wasn't the first person on the planet to struggle in this black hole of *why?* And I surely wouldn't be the last. But, right at this moment I felt completely alone in a dark room behind a locked door, and I couldn't remember what I'd done with the key. Yet, I would have to find a way out. I had no choice. Roger's parents would be devastated. He was an only child, the fair-haired son. They would be depending on me. I was all they had left now.

Can you spell poor bastards, boys and girls?

My breath caught on a sob, and Kane reached out and pulled me into his arms. I pushed ineffectually at his broad chest, suffocating in the fragrant softness of his flannel clad pecs. Even the vague whiff of jelly doughnuts didn't help. I didn't want his sympathy, I didn't need his comfort. He'd known the truth. He'd known and he'd kept it to himself. He didn't care about me, he didn't care about Roger. Why should he? He barely knew me, and Roger was just another soul. He'd had his own agenda all along, and I'd unwittingly fallen right in with his plans and rescued his Hellhound girlfriend from Cerberus. He should have told me. He should have—

"Logan!"

His voice slammed into my head like a shot. I suddenly became aware I'd gone from poodle to pitbull in less than thirty seconds. Pounding on his chest, kicking at his shins, and screaming in his face. The meltdown he'd obviously anticipated arrived with a vengeance and without warning. Hell, even I hadn't seen it coming. Did I mention I didn't do tears and emotion and angst? Not in public and definitely not in front of the Grim Reaper? Hmm, well maybe I'd given myself a little too much credit. I know, it surprised me too, but since I'd already shot my former theory to hell I decided I may as well go with it. I pulled my arm back and my fist came up with my full weight behind it, directly under his chin. His head snapped back like a Pez dispenser. Act like a woman, but hit like a man, Dad always said. I think the strength of the impact surprised us both, and suddenly all of the fight went out of me. After all, I had nothing left to fight for.

While the Grim Reaper rubbed his chin, I discovered two things. One, tears are easier than I thought, and two, it's next to impossible to maintain any degree of dignity with rivers of snot streaming out of your nose.

"Feel better?" Morgan asked, slowly working his jaw back and forth. People always underestimate short people, but we're stronger than we look.

He reached around to his back pocket and then pushed a handkerchief into my hand. I blew my nose and mopped at eyes that felt as though someone had worked them over with a cheese grater.

"You knew, Kane," I repeated tiredly. "I know you don't owe me anything, but you knew and you didn't tell me. Why didn't you tell me?"

"Roger McCoy died last night, Logan," Morgan said gently. "He died and he had unfinished business. That unfinished business was you. He wanted you to have the chance to say good-bye. He wanted some assurance you would be all right. Yes, I knew. And yes I could have told you. It was a judgment call, and I thought it was the right decision at the time. Obviously you disagree and I can understand that. But, supposing I *had* told you, Logan? What would you have done differently?"

That pulled me up short. What *would* I have done differently if I'd known the truth at the onset? Nothing. I would have done exactly the same thing. I still would have gone to the Between. I still would have saved Dirk Kramer. Probably. Oh, hell. Yeah, of course I would have. Roger knew me too well. My conscience wouldn't have let me leave him behind no matter how much he made my skin crawl. I still wouldn't have given up until I'd found Roger. I still would have stubbornly believed I could save him. And I still would have failed. I could move between worlds, I could maybe undo wrongs, but when it came to cheating death I was just as powerless as anyone else.

And what if I wasn't a Retriever? I would have gone to bed last night and woken up this morning as blissfully unaware my world was about to come crashing down as everyone else in the world facing the unthinkable. Knowing wouldn't have changed a thing.

Every scenario I envisioned resulted in the same outcome. Roger was gone. Knowing ahead of time probably wouldn't have made it any easier. Keeping the truth from me had been deliberate, but it hadn't been malicious. Like Kane said, it was a judgment call. It was painful to admit he might have been right. I wanted to blame him. I wanted to blame Alicia. I wanted to blame Dirk. Hell, I wanted to blame someone. Mostly I wanted to stop blaming myself.

I tucked the handkerchief into the breast pocket of his shirt and only then realized the fingers of my other hand were still locked onto his windpipe. He didn't say a word. Then again, it was possible my intractable grip was beginning to hinder his ability to speak. I loosened my hold on his throat and flexed my fingers. Let's be clear, it wasn't like I could do any real damage to a Hellhound Grim Reaper who topped me by over a foot and a half and outweighed me by at least two hundred pounds. But now I'd regained some measure of composure, I had to admit it was nice of him to let me try.

I dug in my pocket and pulled out his watch. I stuffed it into his shirt with the sopping handkerchief. Then I made a move to step away, and this time he didn't try to stop me. I snagged the mug from the table where I'd left it and collapsed back onto the sofa. The coffee was nearly cold by this time, but as we have already established, I am a coffee slut and the diminishing temperature made no difference to me. I chugged it down without difficulty. I still felt awful, but the pending hysteria lurking just below the surface was gone. It had been replaced by a hollow ache that I knew wouldn't be going away any time soon, but at least I felt like I was back in control. Relief via release was a novel concept, at least to me.

My sister Denise can turn on the waterworks at the drop of a hat. Denise has a PhD in weeping. As much as I love her, I'd always considered her to be a bit of a drama queen. But I couldn't argue with the therapeutic results of my uncontrolled outburst. It was hard to believe that perhaps my little sister had the right idea all along. Maybe sometimes you needed to allow yourself to fall apart before you could think about putting yourself back together again. Of course, I'm not convinced going bat shit crazy and attempting to choke the life out of the Grim Reaper is exactly the way to go either, but maybe somewhere out there is a happy medium.

"More coffee?" Kane asked quietly.

"Yeah." I replied, climbing stiffly to my feet. "Definitely more coffee and lots of it. And I also wouldn't say no to chocolate if you've got it."

The coming hours and the coming days were going to totally suck on more levels than I could even contemplate at the moment. I couldn't avoid it, I knew that, but at least I could fortify myself. In my experience, coffee and chocolate were usually the right answer, regardless of the question.

"I don't have much of a sweet tooth myself." The unmarred corner of Kane's lips curled slightly. He stepped back and indicated I should precede him into the kitchen with a wave of his arm. "But I'd be willing to bet Alia's got a stash somewhere."

Alia. Funny, I'd been so determined to bring her back with me, and then promptly managed to forget all about her. Of course, I had a rather valid excuse. Then again, maybe freeing her was less about her and more about winning the battles I could. That and teaching Cerberus he couldn't outsmart crazy. Still, I wasn't sorry I brought her back even though Blondie apparently belonged to Kane and not to me. I was a little disappointed I wouldn't be getting a dog, but at least someone had gotten a happy ending and Sir Chicken Caesar would never have to know how close he'd come to having his position usurped.

When I stepped into the kitchen and spied the statuesque blonde leaning against the counter, I immediately understood that Alia didn't belong to Kane. She didn't belong to anyone but herself. I'd only known her as a pet and not as a person. My bad. She was even taller, blonder, and more beautiful than my sister Denise. Apparently I was cursed. I was clearly destined to go through life as the token dark gnome in the garden of flaxen elegance.

"Max Logan, I believe you've already met my sister, Alia Kane." Morgan snagged the cup from my nerveless fingers, pushed my unresisting body into a chair, and stepped around his sister to get me a refill.

"Your sister?" I echoed like a brain damaged magpie. "But I thought…"

"Yeah, I know what you thought," Morgan sighed. He knew what I'd thought? How could he possibly know? My confusion must have been apparent in my expression.

"You may have mentioned something about my being a selfish, horny Hellhound whose main concern was retrieving my bitch during your earlier tirade."

"Oh." It was an obvious assumption on my part. Besides, who holds a bereaved woman accountable for anything she might say in a moment of madness? "And for the record, it wasn't a tirade. I don't do tirades. It was a cathartic emotional release brought on by grief and fatigue."

"You say po-tay-to, I say po-tah-to," Kane replied as he plunked the cup of dark roasted nirvana in front of me and pulled out a chair for himself. "I wasn't criticizing. If getting it all out of your system made you feel better, I'm glad. Besides, I owe you, Logan. You managed to do what I couldn't. You brought my sister home."

"What were you doing there in the first place?" I directed my question to Alia who was still leaning against the counter, and who'd been oddly quiet thus far.

"Cerberus was using me to get to Morgan," Alia whispered. "Cerberus fancies himself King of the Hellhounds. He doesn't think any of us should be here on the other side instead of over there working for him. He figured he could use me to lure Morgan back to the Between."

"He can come here?" I looked wildly from one to the other. I hadn't exactly endeared myself to the Guardian of Hell. I had enough to deal with at the moment without him deciding it was payback time for Retrievers.

"No, not unless a young and impulsive Hellhound who thinks she knows more than her older and more experienced brother decides to go visiting against direct orders and then forgets to close the portal behind her when she comes home," Morgan interjected in a tight voice.

"I've said I was sorry a million times, Morgan. I

was wrong. Aren't you ever going to forgive me?" Alia cried forlornly.

"I'm just glad you're home and still in one piece, Alia," he replied. "And we owe that to Logan, here. She wants chocolate. Give it up. I know you have some hidden around here somewhere."

Alia levered herself away from the counter and headed for the doorway on the side of the fireplace. She paused beside my chair.

"Thank you, Max. You were awesome over there. Retrievers never stand up to Cerberus. They usually just run away when he shows up. Even the oldest and most experienced would never have crossed him and taken me out from under his nose the way you did. I'm sorry about Roger. After everything you did for the asshat and for me, it doesn't seem fair you shouldn't get a happy ending too."

She leaned over and hugged me quickly then turned and disappeared into the hall. At least she refrained from licking my face this time.

"Asshat?" Kane hid his smile behind the rim of his mug, but I heard it in his voice.

"Dirk," I clarified with a sigh. "I may have verbalized my opinion once or twice in front of your sister. Of course, I didn't realize she was your sister at the time."

"She was with the old woman?"

I nodded. "Apparently she noticed your scent on me and nominated herself my trusty sidekick."

Kane shook his head. "She never learns. I got word she'd escaped Cerberus and managed to get to the Timekeeper. She knew she was safe there until I could figure something out."

"If you can cross over, why didn't you go in and get her back yourself?"

"I tried. Cerberus was waiting. It didn't turn out so well."

"Your scars."

"Yeah."

"She blames herself, you know."

"Probably. But I'd do it again." He picked up his cup and drained it. His Adam's apple bobbed along the smooth column of his throat. Then he plunked the cup back on the table and simply watched me.

"So would I." I replied softly, surprised to realize it was true. The experience had been beyond strange, scary as hell, and ultimately heartbreaking, but even knowing the outcome, I would do it again. I didn't know if Roger had been right about having the chance to say good-bye making it any easier, but at least I had been able to see for myself that if he hadn't yet found peace exactly, he'd found acceptance. Roger had always been much better with directions than I could ever hope to be. He'd successfully navigated Kubler-Ross to its conclusion and was free. In the difficult days to come when the loss seemed too much to bear, I suspected this was what I would cling to when trying to find my way.

Morgan got up and brought the coffeepot over to the table, refilling first my cup and then his before carrying it back to the counter and starting another pot. I decided he was very astute for a Grim Reaper who probably spent half of his time in the guise of a large, black Irish Wolfhound and smelling like wet dog.

Alia shuffled back into the kitchen precariously balancing an alarmingly diverse collection of chocolate treats. I wondered if I should suggest Kane sign her up for a twelve step program. Of course, as a woman whose coffee habit would persuade me to take a bullet for the barista at the Bountiful Bean, I guess I didn't have a lot of room to talk. She dumped everything in the middle of the table and snagged a candy bar for herself. I selected a package of chocolate covered sandwich cookies and ripped into the cellophane with my teeth. I'd just dunked the first cookie in my coffee and popped it into my mouth when my cell phone trilled from the region of my right buttock.

My eyes flew to Morgan's in alarm as I chewed rapidly and reached behind me to yank it free. I checked the display, and my eyes immediately filled.

"Roger's father," I announced dully.

"Next of kin?" Morgan guessed. I nodded. For thirteen years I'd been Roger's next of kin, but after the divorce, he'd designated his father. I guess he'd never bothered to change it back when he gave me Power of Attorney. It was just as well. I'm not sure I could have broken the news to his folks myself. Selfish? Yeah, maybe, but I prefer to think of it as recognizing my own limitations.

I wondered what would happen if I simply didn't answer. Actually, I knew what would happen. He would call my father next. He would call my father and break the news, and my entire family would know Roger was gone before I even got home. They would have time to compose themselves, and I could concentrate on nursing my own broken heart and not have to hold it together while I broke theirs. Actually, the more I thought about it, the more I thought it was a dandy plan. Later I could think about the McCoys.

151

Later I would put them first and do whatever I could to lessen their burden. I owed it to Roger, and it was the right thing to do. But, right now I knew that I needed to do for me or I would be completely useless to everyone else. I shoved the phone back into my pocket and swallowed the guilt along with rest of my cookie. At the risk of being redundant, self-preservation is a strong motivator.

"You can't run from it forever, Logan," Kane said quietly. He reached over and squeezed my hand.

"I know. I…" It suddenly dawned on me I couldn't really avoid it any longer at all. I had to get home. I'd texted Denise last night to say I'd gone to meet Roger. They were about to get a call telling them Roger was dead. I had to let them know I wasn't with him, I was okay. I whipped out my phone and frantically dashed off a message to Denise telling her the truck had broken down, I'd missed my flight, and I was on my way home. I shoved the phone back into my pocket and reached for a handful of chocolate covered pretzels. I crammed them into my mouth until it was so full that I was in danger of dislocating my jaw. Alia simply stared in disbelief. Amateur. Morgan simply waited until I'd washed it all down with the cup of coffee he'd just topped off, then he arched a brow in my direction.

"Ready to go home, Retriever?"

"Not even close to ready, Reaper. But I guess I'm going anyway."

Chapter Ten

As Morgan swung the nose of his truck into the driveway my throat went dry. Denise's sparkling, cobalt X5 luxury SUV leered at me. Brad-the-Famous-Vascular-Surgeon's low slung sports car was parked in front of it. Even my father's beat up blue pick-up with Logan's Hardware stenciled in white on the door was parked at the curb.

Hail, hail, the gang's all here.

In an unusual flash of brilliance, I'd texted Denise again on the way home to say I'd spoken to Roger's dad. It was a bald faced lie, but I figured it would save my family the painful anticipation of wondering how they were going to break the news to me when I got there.

See, I can be thoughtful.

As soon as I opened the door of the truck, my family rushed out of the house like a herd of wildebeest. I knew they meant well, but frankly, moving in a pack like that they were a little scary. Clinique, Denise's Petit Basset Griffon Vendéen, howled frantically at the kitchen door. Her finer sensibilities had obviously been completely offended at being left behind. Clinique is a bit outspoken. She likes to howl. She howls alone, she howls with friends, she howls to music, she howls at being left alone. Sometimes I honestly believe she howls for the cheap thrill of hearing herself howl. She loves me. I don't know why, but she does. As my eardrums vibrated painfully, I wondered what on earth had possessed me to think I might like to have a dog. It must have been a transient ischemic attack of some sort. Either that, or plain old temporary insanity. I slid to the ground and stood there, hanging onto the open door of the Grim Reaper's impressively decked out four-by-four for dear life. I felt like a twig stuck in a ravine watching the approach of a flash flood and helpless to get out of the way.

"You can do this, Logan," Morgan Kane said in a hushed undertone from his place in the driver's seat.

"Of course I can," I replied automatically. I turned and offered him my best deer caught in the headlights smile.

"Would you like to come in?"

Stepmother Gail would do cartwheels if she could hear that. Even with a brain reduced to the consistency of tapioca, I'd remembered my manners. I knew there were times she'd positively despaired I would ever acquire any. But that was last month, this was the new me.

I glanced at Morgan waiting for his answer or maybe hoping for an extra dose of moral support, but he was staring straight ahead, his eyes locked on my father. And my father had stopped dead in his tracks wearing an expression of complete and utter shock. His gaze moved from Morgan to me and back again, and then the color drained from his face. I wouldn't have put Morgan Kane at more than a few years older than me, but apparently he carried his age well because it was clear my father recognized him, and my mother had died over thirty years ago. Oh yeah, my father knew exactly who had delivered me back to the bosom of my family. His baby girl had been hanging with the Grim Reaper.

"Maybe another time," Kane finally responded.

My father's eyes were pretty much bugging out of his head now, and the color rushed back into his face until he resembled an eggplant. Frankly, he didn't look so good.

"Reaper," I began in a worried voice. "You don't have my father on your to-do list anytime soon, do you?"

"No, Logan. Your father is safe from me for the foreseeable future," he laughed.

"Thanks. Just checking."

"Listen, I'd better get going. I don't do crowds, and my presence here will just cause unwanted questions. You have enough to deal with." The transmission clicked as he shifted into reverse, and I stepped clear to close the door.

"Call if you need anything."

"I will. Thanks."

He continued to stare at me intently as though he was trying to put together the pieces of a puzzle. It was getting a little unnerving the way he fixed his gaze on me all the time. Then he nodded shortly, as though he'd satisfied himself about something and sat back against the seat. He gunned the engine and was back in the street even before Denise had launched herself into my arms.

"Oh, Max," she sobbed pitifully. "My poor baby. I'm so, so sorry." Then she lifted her head and watched Morgan's retreating vehicle. "Who was that?"

Distractible? Denise? Well, let's just say I usually tried to avoid waving shiny objects around her.

"Oh, um, he's the mechanic from the garage where I left the truck," I lied. Satisfied, she resumed her sobbing. I hugged her briefly and then put her away from me and headed right for my father who'd finally started moving in my direction again. My pace quickened as I approached him. He opened his arms. I flew into them, and they closed around me—giving me more comfort than he could possibly know. He'd been where I was now, and he came through on the other side well and whole. He'd rebuilt his life, and he'd found happiness again. I might have inherited my supernatural superpowers from my mother, but I also shared fifty percent of my father's DNA. Knowing he'd been able to pick up the pieces gave me hope I could do it, too.

"Was that…?" He choked out.

"Morgan Kane, the Grim Reaper. Yes, Daddy, it was. It's a long story. We can talk about it later."

"Ah, baby girl, I'm so sorry. I'm so sorry about Roger, so sorry about everything."

"I know you are. It's okay, Daddy," I said as his tears mingled with my own. "It's gonna be okay."

"I never wanted this for you. Your mother never wanted this for you."

"Well, Dad," I said with a watery smile. "I guess maybe we both know that what we want usually has absolutely nothing to do with what we get." I squeezed his thick middle, wiped my eyes on my sleeve, and braced myself to greet the rest of my family.

"That's probably true, baby girl," my dad whispered into my hair as Gail and Denise approached with arms outstretched. "But sometimes what we get is not only more than we knew we wanted, sometimes it's exactly what we need. We just have to recognize it when it comes along."

****

I opened my eyes the next morning to golden combs of sunlight streaming through the slats of the wooden shutters. For a moment I reveled in the luxury of the temporary amnesia of sleep. I should have known it was too good to last. I stretched and yawned and rolled to the side of my bed, but found Caesar curled up against me. Not Roger. And then I remembered. It would never be Roger again. That empty ache took up residence in my chest and settled in for a nice long visit. I was slightly surprised to discover morning arrived in exactly the same fashion it always had. I suppose I was experiencing that strange phenomenon peculiar to the bereaved. My world had changed forever, while at the same time the rest of the world had remained exactly the same.

I stacked the pillows behind my head and pulled the covers up to my chin, wanting to avoid this new day for as long as I could. Somehow at the moment, it seemed less painful to look back than to anticipate the days to come. I pulled my cat into my arms and showered him with belly rubs and ear scratches. He's nearly twelve. I failed to consider that the shock of my sudden tender attention might kill him. Fortunately, he possessed enough inherent apathy to survive the suffocating devotion. Poor kitty. Once upon a time he'd been *our* cat. Roger thought smoked salmon and sushi were appropriate kitty treats, and never showed up empty handed. Caesar was going to miss Roger, too.

Sir Chicken Caesar tolerated my unexpected affection for approximately thirty-seven and a half seconds. Then he sank his four remaining teeth into the pad of my thumb, leapt from the bed, and stalked off in search of his breakfast. His tail switching in annoyance. Smart ass! He might think he was the king of the castle, but I had custody of the can opener so he could just sit there and sulk until I was good and ready. I wrapped a crumpled tissue around my bleeding hand and slid out of bed wondering why I ever thought I was a cat person in the first place.

I decided to borrow a page from Roger's Procrastinator's Bible and spend at least thirty minutes standing under the steaming spray of the showerhead. I knew eventually I would have to get out and face the music, but I didn't have any sense of urgency. If there was any justice at all, coffee and jelly doughnuts would be offered before too much was expected of me. The phone started ringing less than three minutes after I got into the shower, and kept ringing every few minutes thereafter. I stuck my head back under the water and tuned it out. I'd had my fill of deadlines in the Between. For the foreseeable future I was determined not to follow anyone's schedule but my own. Whoever it was could call back or they could leave a message. That's why God invented voice mail.

Finally I was forced to accept the fact that no matter how long I stood there, I was not going to dissolve and follow the swirling soap bubbles between the vinyl sticky fish down the drain. I hauled my chunky butt out and wrapped it in the comfort of one of the new bath towels Denise had brought along with her yesterday as a bereavement gift.

I padded back into the bedroom and dug listlessly through my underwear drawer, deliberately burying anything even remotely racy in the back corner. I couldn't imagine any occasion for which I'd need it anytime soon. I snagged a pair of simple cotton Grammy pants, poked my feet through the leg holes, and wiggled them up over my hips. Then I covered them with a clean pair of jeans and a T-shirt. I topped the entire freshly laundered ensemble with Roger's ratty sweater. It looked as though it had been to hell and back, which technically I guess it nearly had. I scraped my wet hair back into a thick ponytail which pretty much guaranteed I'd be sporting a bad seventies afro when it dried. Denise would probably pitch a fit. Then again, watching Denise at full throttle might be an entertaining distraction.

My phone was still on the nightstand where I'd tossed it last night after visiting with Roger's parents. To say it wasn't a pleasant visit would be an understatement. They were completely devastated, just as I'd expected they would be. When I left them I was both sad and angry. Sad for their grief, and angry at Roger that while he was out there lounging by a lake basking in his acceptance of the fickle finger of fate, I was the one left behind to deal with the fallout. Intellectually, I knew it wasn't his fault, but I was in mourning, damn it. I didn't have to be reasonable or fair.

I picked up my phone and checked the display. Denise had called six times, and the stores wouldn't even be open for another two hours. Of course with my sister's credit limit, it was entirely possible that they might be willing to open early specifically for her. We were going shopping to find me the latest in fashionable funeral wear. Denise's idea, not mine. I told her I could dress myself. She would not be dissuaded. Despite her impressive resume of continuing education credits in psychology, her primary and most successful coping mechanism is, and always has been, retail therapy.

I shuffled out to the kitchen and discovered Caesar had parked his oversized bulk directly in front of his blue ceramic bowl with the little white paw prints. As I came around the island and turned on the coffeemaker, I swear he reached out one little gray paw and pushed it pointedly in my direction.

"Feel entitled, much?" I groused while digging in the utensil drawer. I opened a can of tuna surprise and upended it in his dish. He sniffed the lump of gelled fish bits haughtily, then lumbered to his feet and strolled casually out of the kitchen and over to the patio doors, where he collapsed in a patch of sun and promptly began to snore.

"Ingrate," I mumbled. I'd just filled my super-sized *I'm Having One of Those Decades* coffee mug and taken that first satisfying and sanity restoring sip when unbelievably the phone trilled again. For the space of a heartbeat I considered ignoring it and using the excuse I didn't answer because I was dancing along with my ringtone and got carried away. It had happened before. Then I decided it was probably in poor taste under the circumstances.

"For the love of Pete, Denise! The mall doesn't even open for two more hours. Can't a grieving girl at least have a cup of coffee before she's dragged off to be tortured?" I shouted into the phone without bothering to check the screen.

"Logan?" The rich, honeyed voice crawling into my bone marrow most definitely did not belong to my sister. Oops. My bad.

"Kane? Sorry, I thought you were my sister."

"Oh. I just wanted to see how you were holding up. And to tell you the Timekeeper sent cookies."

"She did? Really? Gee, that was nice of her. How about the gin? Did she send the gin?"

"Huh?"

"Never mind. Inside joke. Could you please thank her for me? I wouldn't have a clue as to where to address a thank you card. I'm pretty sure the postal service doesn't have the Between on any of its regular routes. Listen, why don't you and Alia keep them? The last time I checked there was already enough food next door at my father's to feed a third world country."

"There is? Why?" He sounded genuinely puzzled.

"Why? Well, because that's what people do. When someone dies, they cook, they bake, they send indecent amounts of paper products and sandwich rolls to the family homestead. For a Grim Reaper you really haven't bothered to keep up to speed on routine human death etiquette, have you?"

"I guess not. Doesn't really fall under my job description. Well, anyway I thought I should tell you about the cookies."

"Oh, uh, yeah, thanks. Um, Morgan, while I've got you on the phone, I've been wondering about something."

"What's that?"

"Was it you? Roger, I mean. Were you the one who…" I couldn't quite get the words *severed Roger's soul* to pass my lips, but I knew the Grim Reaper would get my drift. All in all, Morgan Kane struck me as a pretty bright guy, although you'd never know it from the size of *his* hips. I guess he just didn't need to display his superior intelligence as blatantly as I did. He didn't answer right away, and I knew that was an answer in itself even before I heard the quiet response.

"Yes."

"I'm glad." I swallowed so hard that I think he probably heard it on his end.

"You're...glad?" He sounded like he was choking on something. Maybe he decided to start chomping on the cookies already?

"Well, I mean someone had to do it, right? At least knowing it was you, well I feel kind of like at least it was someone who...I don't know...cared? Well, I don't mean cared, exactly. More like a friend. Well, maybe not really a friend." I took a deep breath and reigned myself in. "What I mean is, I'm glad it wasn't just some indifferent supernatural being slinging a big nasty scythe around all willy-nilly, ya know?"

"It's my job, Logan."

"I know, it's just...well, anyway, thanks. For calling, I mean. Enjoy the cookies."

"I told you I don't have—"

"Oh, that's right, you don't have a sweet tooth. Well, at least your sister will enjoy them."

"I guess so." He lapsed into silence, and I was running low on witty small talk.

"Well..." We both began at the same time and then laughed self-consciously.

"If there's anything I can do, Logan..."

"There's isn't. It's just something I have to navigate myself, but thanks."

"Okay, then…" he trailed off awkwardly as though maybe he wanted to say more, but he didn't.

"'Bye, Reaper."

"So long, Retriever. Take care of yourself." And the line went dead.

I wondered if he bothered to check up on all of the bereaved survivors of his clients. I was betting he didn't. Maybe it was because I was a kind of co-worker in a strange and not completely clear sort of supernatural way. Or maybe it was because I was the first bereft survivor that ever had a meltdown in his arms and then tried to strangle him. Either way, I thought it was nice of him to make the effort.

Chapter Eleven

The funeral was extremely well attended. Roger was a popular guy. Friends, family, colleagues—the line of mourners was endless, or so it seemed to me. I still couldn't believe I was using the words funeral and Roger in the same sentence. Then again, I guess most people in my position feel that way. I just wanted to go home. I wanted to wrap myself in my sorrow and Roger's Aran sweater, and somehow find the strength to accept the things I knew I couldn't change.

Speaking of Roger's sweater, initially I'd taken it off only to shower. My family regarded me oddly, more oddly than usual anyway. What they didn't know was when I buried my face in that sweater and closed my eyes, I could still smell Roger. I knew eventually his scent, like everything else, would fade. Well, maybe not everything. There were other scents associated with filthy, damp wool that were not fading. In fact, they had begun to reach the point of nauseating. Denise pointed out my ensemble would be construed by some as disrespectful to Roger's memory. She might also have mentioned something related to questionable personal hygiene. I admit sometimes I have trouble seeing the forest for the trees. Luckily for me my sister is always willing to slam my head into a tree trunk to help me out. That's what family is for. At least that's how she spins it. She was the personal stylist behind the sophisticated black sheath I currently wore. She was right as usual. Roger would have loved me in it.

My elderly former in-laws huddled together in anguished disbelief near the head of the closed casket. They were so distraught, I initially considered telling them the truth, hoping it would provide them with some measure of peace. Then I decided they'd probably call in a bunch of specialists, agree I'd finally snapped under the strain, and have me committed, which probably wouldn't have made them feel any better in the long run. It wouldn't have done me much good, either.

The McCoys had asked me to handle the arrangements, and I did it with a vengeance, sparing no expense. I admit I may have gone a little over the top but in my mind, Roger deserved the biggest, most ostentatious sendoff I could engineer. After all of the arguments I'd instigated regarding my alimony, it turns out money really means less than nothing at all. I know there are those who will argue it's easy for me to say now that I was in a position where I didn't need to worry about finances. Well, I'll see their argument and raise them an all-the-money-in-the-world-can't-bring-him-back. In retrospect, I think all the bickering about alimony was just an excuse I used to maintain contact when we were apart. I like to think he knew that even if it took me a little longer to catch on.

With my father on one side and my stepmother on the other, I greeted the visitors with dry-eyed composure and few words. Everyone presumed I was still in shock. The truth of the matter was, my grief had become a quiet constant that ran too deep for tears or tongue. I'm told there's a point where you're so numb you can't even feel pain anymore. I looked forward to that state of being.

People were kind. Some offered words of inspiration. Some choked up and simply held me to convey their sorrow. Some had a funny story about Roger to share, and we all smiled awkwardly. It was nice to remember, but it was painful to know that there wouldn't be any more memories to make. Memories were lovely, but they were finite. And then there were the people who simply came for show. Those were the people I found myself agreeing with only to encourage them to stop talking and move on. They meant well, every single one of them. I knew it. Most of them would have done anything for me. I knew that, too. But the bitter truth was, when this day ended, they would all go home and their lives would go on exactly the same as they had before. Mine was profoundly and irrevocably changed. I felt like a drowning victim gazing up from the depth of the murky water and watching everyone else breathe.

I might have been the one person present who knew beyond a shadow of a doubt Roger's soul continued on somewhere. The fact that the somewhere wasn't here with me was the piece of the equation that I still wrestled with. I would never again feel his arms snake around me when I woke in the night, would never see his eyes crinkle with laughter over the morning paper, and I would never attend a social function and feel my heart swell with pride when that charming, sexy man across the room caught my eye and gave me that slow, sweet smile that was pure Roger. Every time I heard a funny story, or had a random idea, and thought *I have to tell Roger,* I would never be able to pick up the phone and share it. He wouldn't be there to hear it. There were too many nevers. It hurts to have someone in your heart, and not your arms.

I spied Dirk being wheeled in by Nancy, his leg caged in an external fixator. I had no idea how much, if anything, he remembered. I only knew I didn't want to deal with it right now. As soon as there was a break in the line, I excused myself, and quietly snuck out a side door. I parked myself against the railing and just let myself breathe. I couldn't face him, not yet. I knew it was neither his fault nor mine, but I still struggled to accept the inequity of what felt like his survival at Roger's expense. I told you, I'm grieving. I don't have to be reasonable.

Love, anger, and admiration all vied for dominance in my heart when I considered Roger's calm acceptance of his fate. I knew the love would prevail in the end, but there were moments when a part of me wanted to punch Roger square in the face. Hard. Isn't that what you do when someone breaks your heart? And then you go lock yourself in a room and eat chocolate.

I worry that Roger was wrong about me. I think I was quite capable of making the selfish choice. I'm not so sure I wouldn't have offered Dirk up on a silver platter in Roger's place if the option had been offered to me. But I also know that if I hadn't been strong enough to do the right thing, Roger would have been. Roger wouldn't have made the selfish choice because if he had he wouldn't be Roger. He would be less somehow. He would be Dirk. And wasn't that a hell of a paradox?

My brother-in-law told me yesterday that Dirk's youngest daughter had just been diagnosed with leukemia. She's only twelve years old. Roger had said

Nancy was going to need Dirk. Maybe things really did happen for a reason. I couldn't imagine the devastation of losing a child you'd borne, held, and loved. No one should ever have to bear it once, let alone face it twice. Some days there just aren't enough rude gestures in the world.

I heard the low buzz of conversation as the door opened and closed behind me. The weight of a coat settled over my shoulders. The wooden railing creaked as someone leaned beside me. I didn't even have to look to know it was my father. We'd had a long talk last night after everyone else was asleep. He'd never told me the truth because he and my mother had been assured the binding could never be broken. No one counted on a snot-nosed G.R.I.T. with purple braces and a chip on his shoulder. I couldn't think about Buddy right now. In fact, I'd really like it a lot if I couldn't think about anything at all. I hadn't touched a cigarette in over three months, but I could sure use one at the moment. Then again, what would it solve?

"How ya holding up, kiddo?" My father lightly bumped his shoulder into mine. He'd never been the most demonstrative man. I shrugged. My throat ached with unshed tears, but there didn't seem to be much point in making a spectacle of myself. All the tears in the world wouldn't change anything. Been-there-done-that and Roger was still gone. Crying would only make my face blotchy and my eyes puffy. Not to mention Denise would insist on dragging me to the ladies room to repair the damage. Appearances were important to her. Don't get me wrong, I'm not judging. Everyone has their own way of coping. I just think I was still looking for mine.

"You know, honey," my big strapping dad began in a choked voice. "Being able to say goodbye is a great gift. I had that with your mom, just like you did with Roger. Not everyone is so lucky."

"Does it help?" I whispered. Roger had thought it would. So far I wasn't sure I'd reaped any benefit. My dad slung a beefy arm across my shoulders and hugged me tight against his side. He heaved a heavy sigh.

"Not today. Not tomorrow. But eventually, baby girl. Eventually. You just gotta fake it till you make it."

We stood together in the companionable silence of shared grief and embraced the night. Cars continued to stream into the parking lot, and I knew we were going to be here a lot longer than the hours posted for visitation. I figured I should probably check on Roger's folks and see if they needed anything. Dad and I slipped back inside. Roger's aunt and her brood had arrived from Chicago and surrounded my former in-laws. They would be fine for now. Dirk and Nancy had already gone through the line, offered their condolences, and made an exit. I'm sure they wondered where I was, but I couldn't bring myself to care. I was off the hook for the moment. I would give Nancy a call in a couple of days and see how things were going.

Gail hurried over and asked if I needed a drink. I sure did, but the water she handed me probably wasn't going to cut it. When this was all over, my friend Jose Cuervo and I were going to curl up together for a nice long visit. Unconsciousness and memory loss—the free prize in the bottom of every bottle of tequila. I disentangled myself from my father's arm, stood on tiptoe, and kissed him on the cheek. Then I loosened his tie. He wasn't a formal kind of guy and frankly he looked like he was in danger of strangling. I wasn't as hung up on appearances as Denise. Breathing was more important, and it was the thought that counted.

"Thank you, Daddy. I love you." He hadn't known how to help me when I'd gone through my divorce, but he'd really tried to step up to the plate this time. Loss, grief, the capriciousness of fate—those things he understood only too well. My mother had only been thirty-four when we'd lost her.

"I love you, too, baby girl," he said gruffly. "I love you, too."

The crowd finally thinned out a bit and everyone seemed to be occupied. I stepped up to the casket and laid my hand upon the gleaming surface. Roger wasn't in there. I knew it better than anyone. Still, I wanted to touch...what? I really didn't know. Masses of flowers fought for attention all around the bier. The cloying, overpowering scent of their mingled and competing perfumes was something I knew I would never forget and would always associate with pain and loss. They were beautiful, I suppose, but ultimately meaningless. In a few days they would be dead, too. There were some sent with true thought behind them, of course, but many others were sent out of nothing more than a sense of duty or obligation. I couldn't help thinking how drab they would appear in the monochromatic landscape of the Between.

Finally this night I thought would never end actually did. I kissed Roger's parents good-night, told them I would see them in the morning for the funeral, and piled into the limo with the rest of my family. Brad-the-Famous-Vascular-Surgeon had insisted on renting the car so we could all ride together. At the moment I was really looking forward to just getting back to my apartment and being alone. It was incredibly thoughtful of him though. I promised myself I wouldn't make any cracks about his black socks and sandals until at least mid-August.

Back at the house, everyone climbed out and headed for my father's. I hung back and Gail turned to me with a worried frown.

"Are you okay, honey?"

"I'm just really tired. I think I'm going to head upstairs and try to get some sleep. Tomorrow's going to be another long day."

"I understand, Maxine. Wait here one minute, will you?" Gail hurried off before I had a chance to answer. I was really going to hold her to that one minute thing. If I didn't get these shoes off soon, I might never walk again. I should have known it was too much to hope Denise would select flats for my stylish funerary ensemble. Denise fashion rule number one—beauty is pain. My feet hurt so much I figured I must be freakin' gorgeous. On the upside, I'd completely forgotten about my ankle and knee. Gate control theory, remember?

True to her word, Gail bustled out of the house in a heartbeat carrying a white waxed paper bag and held it out to me.

"Here, I thought you might be hungry later," she said. I didn't have to open the bag. I knew exactly what it contained. My own personal comfort food. I'd never considered Gail my mother. It had always felt vaguely disloyal to my birth mother. But Gail was the one who'd sacrificed for me and stood by me and held my hand through every childhood illness, every teenage breakup, and every adult trauma. I hadn't always made it easy. In fact I sometimes made it downright impossible. Yet, she always managed to love me in spite of myself. And like Roger, she could be gone in the blink of an eye. She'd been my mother in every way that counted, and she deserved to know it. Somehow, I think my mother would understand. And I think she would approve.

"Long Johns?" I smiled. "You know, in case I haven't told you lately, you're the best. Thanks…Mom."

If I live to be a hundred I will never forget the look on her face. It only took one simple word to make up for every rotten thing I'd ever said to her. And it hadn't even killed me. Of course, when the color drained from her face and she hit the ground with a thud, I was a little worried it might have killed *her*. Turns out she had forgotten to eat and had gotten a little hypoglycemic. I kicked off my shoes and sank down on the ground beside her, and we split a Long John in companionable silence. Neither of us seemed to be aware the temperature hovered around forty degrees. It was the most relaxed I'd felt in days. We licked the raspberry jam off our fingers, dusted the coconut crumbs off of our laps, and then I helped her to her feet.

"See you in the morning," I said and pressed my lips to her papery cheek.

"Bright and early," she replied. Then she went into her house, and I picked up my shoes and climbed the daunting stairs to mine. At least my usual leg cramps were overshadowed by the excruciating pain in my feet. I think Gail and I just had a moment. Awkward? Maybe a little. But I felt fairly confident we'd get past it as soon as we both got over the shock.

I'd forgotten to leave a light on, so I fumbled my key into the lock and promptly tripped over the door sash while juggling my shoes and Long Johns and trying to reach inside the wall for the switch. The porch light came on, the shoes went flying, and I landed on my ass. Hard. Seriously? Of course, my descent was preceded by a complicated pirouette that I'm sure looked a lot more graceful than it felt. Caesar had been napping on the chair. He opened one eye and saw it was me. Me, solo. No catnip, kitty treats, or milk. He rolled over and went back to sleep.

Wearily, I pushed the door closed and used the knob to pull myself to my feet. I couldn't remember the last time I'd been this tired. Whose bright idea was it to have a funeral at nine in the morning anyway? Oh, right. That would be me. I'd wanted, no needed, to get it over with. I wasn't counting on what I might feel like on the morning after the night before. Otherwise I probably would have scheduled the service for dinnertime.

I reached behind me and flicked on the kitchen light, and then froze. On the island stood one small, unobtrusive crystal bud vase with an arrangement of flowering dogwood tied with a simple green ribbon. Parked next to the flowers was a bottle of gin. What, no cookies? My throat tightened. It was simple and tasteful and it spoke to me more than all of the exotic and expensive expressions of sympathy fighting to make the biggest impression at the funeral home. Maybe more than anything else could have. The dogwood flower—brief to bloom, healing in nature, and symbolic of sacrifice. It was an appropriate and beautiful tribute to Roger. Then there was the stem—tough and resilient, resistant to injury and permanent damage. That, I knew, was a message for me. I bend but I don't break. There was no card, but there didn't need to be. The Grim Reaper knew I would understand.

I bend but I don't break. Roger had said that, too. I felt as bent as I'd ever been, but I knew there was still a pair of big girl panties lying around somewhere. I'd get around to putting them on. Eventually. But probably not tonight. Until I managed to climb back into them, maybe I could use duct tape to hold everything together.

Letting go is really hard. But so is hanging on. Letting go doesn't mean you love someone less. It means accepting what is. Roger believed it. He wanted me to believe it. I was trying. I knew I couldn't continue to start every day with the broken pieces of yesterday indefinitely. At some point I had to start building a new tomorrow. It wouldn't be the one I'd planned, but that didn't mean it couldn't be one worth looking forward to.

If you plant the same crop in a field year after year, the soil becomes depleted. Sometimes the field has to remain empty for a time to recover and produce something fruitful. Life and death are a cycle, and sometimes you need to plant a different crop or allow yourself a fallow period before you can blossom again. It might be the middle of winter at the moment but spring was right around the corner, and deep down I knew eventually something fresh and green and new would begin to sprout.

I pulled a glass out of the cabinet and cracked open the gin. I clinked my glass against the bud vase and drank a toast to what was, what could have been, and what would never be. I reached out and stroked the silken flower petals. The plant was out of season, its blooms should be impossible, but I think maybe I'm beginning to understand nothing is impossible. Well, except maybe trying to nail pudding to a tree. Good luck with that.

The gift was thoughtful, it was subtle. It was a gentle reminder that gave me hope. It was exactly what I needed. It was perfect. I broke a piece of the dogwood off and tucked it behind my right ear. Then I drank another toast to the future, whatever it might bring.

Sharon Saracino

Don't forget to pick up *Smitten With Death*
the third book in the Max Logan series
Available at The Wild Rose Press

A word about the author...

Award-winning author Sharon Saracino was born and raised in beautiful Northeastern Pennsylvania. Always the girl with her nose in a book, a lifelong love of writing took a back seat to real life while she got married, raised a family, and finally decided what she wanted to be when she grew up. She frequently announced that someday she was going to write a book. One milestone birthday (we won't discuss which one!) she decided someday would be here and gone if she didn't get her butt in gear. She plans to win the lottery just as soon as she remembers to purchase a ticket, fantasizes about moving to Italy, brews limoncello, and believes there's always magic to be found if you only take the time to look for it.

http://sharonsaracino.com

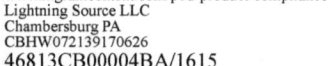